REVENGE AGAINST EVIL

REVENGE

REVENGE

SHEILA CHILSON

ISBN
978-1-958690-37-6 (Paperback)
978-1-958690-38-3 (eBook)
978-1-958690-36-9 (Hardcover)

TABLE OF CONTENTS

CHAPTER 1

The red and golden leaves of a seasons past glories blow across highway 81 which runs along the breath-taking vista of the Shenandoah Valley. The beautiful sight of the hills and valleys spreading out to the sides and front of Gwyn's moving car make her miss her family more. She wants to say, "look over there at x, y, z," to the girls or to her husband, Tom. She wanted to share the many amazing life moments with the people she loved.

The twins, Mazie and Aimee were back at Auburn University for their second year of college. Gwyn had taken a month off from medical practice to get the girls settled into school. This was the longest vacation break she had taken since Tom was reported missing in action. If she had too much time on her hands, she always started the what ifs. As in what if Tom was still alive or what if he was being held prisoner somewhere in the battle scared lands of that wild distant country of Afghanistan.

Gwyn had spent 2 weeks getting the girls settled into their cute, newly built apartment right in the middle of the college campus. Now she had plenty of time for the drive to Virginia to meet two of the widows of Tom's closest military friends. The men had worked as a team from the beginning of their officers training. Tom and Edward Garner were reported missing at the same time during a peace mission in Afghanistan. There was the usual huge explosion, and nothing left to identify. Jack Williams had been reported missing about nine months before them. He had disappeared during some mission high in the mountains, when the Taliban had attacked his group.

Gwyn and her husband Tom met in her first year of college. She was only eighteen, but for her it was love at first sight. Tom was giving a lecture on ethics to pre-med hopefuls. He was finishing his law degree and working as an assistant to a professor, which entailed teaching the less interesting class's.

Tom could not take his eyes off the cute brunet in the front row. She had the greenest eyes he had ever seen. After each lecture she would come up to him with a question and they would eye one another for a moment. On lecture six, with one to go. Tom walked over to Gwyn, who was always early for this class, leaned over and looked hotly into her amazing green eyes and asked if she would go for coffee after class. They had been together every sense.

Tom had made the fun road trip with Gwyn and their daughters to set up the girl's small apartment for their first year of college. He had been gone much of the growing up years. His job as a military negotiator had really kept him on the move all over the world.

When the girls were born, Gwyn was doing her surgical residency at, South Alabama University Medical School. As always Tom was far, far away. She had the twins with her Mom and sister at her side. Gwyn's Mom watched the babies for Gwyn to finish her medical training, which Gwyn did with flying colors. Then, with school behind her, Gwyn and the girls started traveling with Tom and they became a family unit for the first time.

Gwyn worked at the military base hospitals wherever they were stationed. She did everything from delivering babies to gunshot wounds. She was very well rounded in her medical experiences. Gwyn was a state side, emergence rooms dream come true.

The family was living in Guam when Gwyn told Tom that she and the girls were going back home to Birmingham, Alabama. At first Tom was shocked, but after thinking about it, he knew it was the right thing for Gwyn and the girls.

The parts of the world he had been taking his family had no respect for Americans, let alone women. It did not matter what nationality the woman was, they were treated as forth rate citizens or as the possession of some man. The girls needed to be out of harm's way and back in the States for their teen years there they could grow up as strong confident women, like their wonderful Mom.

The girls were to enter six grade and had been to seven different private or military schools with their families' relocations. Gwyn and Tom knew it was time to find a spot to call their own. They bought a large, rambling home in Birmingham. Gwyn's family all lived with-in an hour of the new house.

Tom would fly home after being gone for days and sometimes weeks. He would be exhausted from a month or longer in the Sudan or some other troubled spot in the world. America wanted him to reason with thugs and dictators about how wrong it is to kill their helpless citizens and take their land and positions.

It did not take him long to appreciate the beautiful home that Gwyn had established for them. Tom loved to hunt and fish. He could not ask for a better place to live then, Alabama. It was only a couple of hours drive to The Gulf of Mexico where they could charter a boat, plus the Sea Captain, for fine deep-sea fishing. The rivers and lakes for freshwater fishing were just minutes from them. The weather was wonderful for outside fun year around.

Mazie and Amiee loved their new school and making friends for a lifetime. Gwyn was enjoying her family and her job in the local hospital emergency room. Life had become an easy, wonderful routine for the first time in their lives.

Tom was home a little more. He was working in Washington, D.C. and coming home most weekends. Then, Iraqi happened, and Afghanistan followed. Gwyn could not keep up with his coming and goings at that point. It was hard to believe that the girl's school, proms, and graduation came and went. Time waits for no man or Tom.

Tom could not believe it was time for the girls to go to college. He came home for the fireworks and barbeque of the Fourth of July and found the girls packing up for their first year at The University of Auburn, home of the War Eagle. It was not his and Gwyn's Alma Mater. They both attended the University of Alabama, the States school for law and medicine. The schools have quit the football revelry and Tom and Gwyn had always gone to the big football games between Auburn and Alabama at Thanksgiving each year. How could he cheer for the other team? Tom took it like a champion and loved every minute of being with Gwyn and the girls for this life change. He had missed so many of the steppingstones of all their lives.

Tom felt like a time traveler. He would step into the home in Birmingham from a long flight from somewhere, and the girls would be late for dance class, soccer practice or a date. The last time he was home before the college trip, he arrived in time to see them walk across the football field as twin Home Coming Queens. He was a lucky man and knew it!

Tom and Gwyn had taken their first vacation without the kids after leaving the girls college apartment set up in Auburn. They drove all the way down to Key Biscayne. They played in the beautiful, blue waters of the Gulf of Mexico and lay in the soft, warm sand. They drink margaritas and enjoy wonderful fresh sea food. They also learned how much they had missed each other. One night after making love under the moons silvery glow, Tom made a promise to Gwyn to end his traveling. He knew it would be great in Birmingham with Gwyn. He was ready for a peaceful and fun time in his life. It would take at least a year to end his busy schedule with the military as a negotiator, but he could honestly say he was ready. Life would be amazing.

Just before Christmas break from college for the girls, Tom gets a call. The Army wants him to go to a secret meeting outside of Kandahar, Afghanistan. He assures Gwyn the job will take a week, at the most ten days. It is with some renegade group of the Taliban, who want to give names and locations of dissidents, who have bounty on their heads. Which means, these people are valuable to some country or group dead or alive. The meeting spot has not been well planned out. The unknown thugs have too much control over the time and place.

The military had called in two of their best Marine negotiators, Tom and one of his lifelong friends, Marine Col. Edward Garner. There will be three others putting their lives at risk. Matt Fischer will be the helicopter pilot. Tom always has him fly his missions. Tom knows if you need a fast get away or back up from unexpected trouble, Matt is your man. There is also the co- pilot and gunner that Matt will choose.

They leave Kandahar and head east for this remote location of fact finding. Tom feels very uneasy about the push to go to this meeting so quickly. There have not been enough background checks on the area or the group with which they are dealing. He hates putting good men and himself, into greater whisk by not being assured of the people and place involved. This situation is too dangerous.

As they fly low over the deep, rocky valleys and scenic snow-covered mountain tops. They look down on the occasional village tucked away under the wild growing brush and windblown trees. A group of Children are playing soccer in an open spot close to their homes. The group stop their soccer game and lift waving arms in greetings to the helicopter and crew. It reminds the men that the normal things of life cling to this battle scared land. This is the reason the American peacekeepers travel so far from home and family. They want to bring peace and safety to these families' and tribes.

The tension is quite high as the men near the meeting site. It is a thrown together mission for a talk with thugs with no respect for human life. They had demanded lots of money be delivered to them in paper bags, so they can help the people. Sure, that is who will be helped!

Matt and his helicopter crew really did not know what happened in the small two-story structure. The heavily shawl draped group only allowed Tom, Edward, and the bags of money to get off the helicopter. The explosion happened with-in ten minutes of landing. Matthew though at the time of detonation that it was hotter explosion then it should have been for one small mud hut and two good men.

Matt had been directed to land about 150 yards away from the small structure and at a slightly lower elevation. The helicopter crew's visibility of what was happening on the back side of the building and the surrounding hills was non-existent. This meeting without proper planning or protection was a fiasco.

Gun shots started coming at the chopper from every direction. They had to take off fast or die with the others. The deafening blast turned the building into a red-hot inferno of which no one could have survived. And that was what Matthew Fischer would write in his report.

Tom and Edward were not prepared to go undercover. It was not fair to put their families through such a horrible nightmare. But the choice was not theirs to make.

As Tom stepped away from the helicopter, he though he caught a familiar swaggering walk from the man leading the way. The sand and dirt filling the arid air in a swill around them from the helicopters turning blades restricted his vision. Tom had to squint his eyes to keep the grit out of them. The band of Afghan warriors they were following all looked alike. They were covered with the usual scarves and wool clothing against the bitter cold. The only thing that made them distinguishable from one another was the eyes. Tom recognized the pair that went with the walk.

Jack Williams had been listed as missing in action for about ten months now. As the recognition passed between the two men, a finger to the scarf covered mouth silenced Tom.

They entered the disheveled mud and straw structure and were hurried straight out the back door and into a cave opening about ten feet behind the house. The American voice behind the eyes and walk, yelled, "Move, Move, Move." The group ran a quick hundred-yard sprint, thru a slopping tunnel that had been dug deep into the rocky hill behind the hut. Just as they stepped out into the daylight on the other side, a loud blast rocked the very ground they were standing on. As the last man cleared the tunnel, rocks, dirt, and sand filled the void and the air. Rocks and debris shot out of the collapsing tunnel. They ran down the hillside as sharp bits and pieces of earth, cut into their backs.

Another opening appeared in front of them. They were moving quickly as a group now. Tom and Edward were now committed to whatever was to happen next. They heard the distant gun fire and the helicopter retreating into the hills. Jack said, "Don't ask questions now, I will explain later." Tom and Edward were handed Afghan tribal clothing to change into and their military uniforms and I.D.'s were taken and stuffed into bags that were buried in pre-dug holes in the cave. Tom and Edward came out looking like the locals. All the men mounted tough, small, mountain horses that the region was known for and went off at a hard trot. It had taken about 20 minutes from the time they had stepped off the helicopter for Tom and Edward to enter a different world. As Tom and his pony climbed the rocky path to nowhere, all he could think was "Please God, look after Gwyn." His pony lunged forward as another explosion rocked the ground. Jack had placed enough explosives in the small cave where their cloths were buried to destroy, New York City. It was the cave where they had entered as American military and came out as military militia. It would be a lonely, flipped upside down, spot in time for these men, and torture for their families.

The men rode into the mountains on a trail that fall away to bottomless valleys on one side and the other side rose to snow covered Swiss Alp like mountain ranges. The sure-footed pony moved on in a clop, clop rhythm. Tom had not ridden a horse in years. He sure hoped he could walk after this day long assault on his body.

Jack glances back at Tom and smiles that buccaneer smile that Tom thought he would never see again. At that moment, Tom realizes he is in for the adventure of a lifetime, and he hopes the outcome will be worthy of the pain they were putting their loved ones through.

CHAPTER 2

Gwyn is very tired of driving now and she is trying to remind herself why she had agreed, to this long, lonely road trip.

Her wonderful family in Birmingham had been incredibly supportive of she and the girls through Toms' death and funeral last November. Gwyn's younger twin brothers, Cole and Conner lived with-in six miles of her home. Her mother Bonnie, lived with Cole and his young family. They were in and out of each other lives with visits or phone calls daily. It was always wild and wooly on holidays with school, parties and just the gathering of their great friends and family. It had been a sad time last year for all of them without Tom.

Things were so different for her since the girls were away at college and no Tom. Gwyn hoped this trip would be a closure from Toms' death and not just drag the pain and sorrow up to the surface again. She had worked extremely hard to keep peace with those demons. It was the only way she could keep her emotions and sanity under control.

Allie Garner had called to ask Gwyn to meet with her and Peg Williams at Allies' home in Virginia. Allie reasoned that her home would be about the middle point of travel distance for the two women. Allie had information that she had come about privately on their husbands' disappearance. She wanted to share the info with them.

The word," disappearance," was what had stirred the raw hope inside Gwyn. The missing in action thing would always leave a tiny glimmer of light that would flicker in Gwyn's heart for Tom, forever.

Gwyn had thought about the invitation overnight and then called Allie and accepted, so the date was set. Now, here she was turning off the Interstate to where the glimmer of her heart had brought her. It was only seven miles down a two-lane country road to, "Willow farm," Allies' home. There was almost no traffic at 2:30 on this fall afternoon. Gwyn passed a field of slow moving black and white cows. They were being herded by border collies moving at the speed of light, busily snapping at the heels of the trailers. The cows and dogs were making their way to a large red, milking barn at the top of the gently sloping hill.

Large masses of yellow daises were in full bloom all along the fences and roadside ditches.

As Gwyn rounded a bend in the road, she came to a halt a large yellow school bus. It was flashing its lights and had its red stop signs stuck out to protect its precious cargo from traffic. Two red headed boys of about ten and a willowy girl of twelve, descended from their ride from school and started up the drive that Gwyn was waiting to turn across the road to enter.

A low stone wall with a large brass plate declared this the drive to, "Willow Farm." The kids pulled bikes, hidden on the back side of the wall and made a mad dash for home. There was no house visible from the main road. The old hardwood trees, which lined both sides of the red clay drive, wove a fluttering canopy of red and gold leaves over- head. They spilled down onto Gwyn's car as a gustily puff of wind shook the treetops. She opened the window to breath in the crisp, clean country air. The thick bed of leaves on the drive muffled the sound of her car. She slowed down to a crawl behind the children, to give them a head start for home. After about two hundred yards of woods the drive opened to a large picturesque, two-story house which had been built in the federal style at least 180 years ago. The mellowing brick and cream-colored woodwork made for a great homey feel. A large front porch with rocking chairs pulled you in for a sit in the shade and to stay for a friendly chat.

There was no sight of bikes or children. The threesome had ridden to the back entrance of the house where Gwyn bet there was a snack waiting in the kitchen for them.

Gwyn parked in front of the house and turned off her car. She sat for a moment to enjoy the beauty and quiet around her. She had hopes for the first time, that this journey would bring her a safer and more peaceful place in her mind. She needed answers that hopefully Allie knew. Then she could move on with her life. She felt a satisfying excitement, as if something wonderful was about to happen. And it was.

The three children Gwyn had seen getting off the school bus suddenly spilled out the front door of the big house and came smiling up to her car. Just as she opened the car door to greet them, a tall pretty blond, obviously their mom, stepped out onto the porch. She called for Gwyn to let the kids carry her bags and things into the house. The happy crew collected her things and as she turned to follow the happy trio, her cell phone started an odd jingle ring. As she pulled it from her jacket pocket, a cold, sharp wind came howling down the driveway behind her and sent a chill through her bones. A series of unfamiliar numbers appeared on her phone. They were 3579 press y answer now. Since when did cell phones start getting pushy? Allie and Gwyn exchanged a quick smile and eye contact just as Gwyn pressed y. Toms' voice started telling her that he was ok. Not to worry. He, Jack, and Edward were fine, and they needed she and the other wives to help them with a mission. They would contact them tonight at Allies house. Tom said, "I love you, please forgive me." There was a click and then nothing.

Allie was watching Gwyn from the front porch and knew immediately who the phone call was from. She had already gotten that shocking, but life renewing call from Edward. Allie ran to Gwyn who was standing frozen to the spot with the phone still at her ear. She put her arm around Gwyn's' shoulders and walked her up the steps and into the house. The kids had taken Gwyn's' things to the front guest bedroom upstairs. Allie led Gwyn through the large front hallway of the old house. It had a beautiful curving staircase and wonderful family portraits lining the walls. An open door at the back of the hallway led them into a warm and inviting family room with a large, attached kitchen. Allie took Gwyn to an overstuffed chair by the fireplace and told her to sit for a bit. It was scary how deathly pale Gwyn looked. Allie went to the kitchen and pulled a bottle of apricot brandy out of the top cupboard, mixed a double shot of it with milk, warmed it in the microwave for 30 seconds and put it in Gwyn's' hand and said, "take a drink." Gwyn took a sip, and then a bigger one. The strong drink with the deep flavor sent a warm feeling through her body and the sound of his voice came back to her. Tears started spilling down her face. Gwyn took another long swallow and started telling Allie about the cruel trick or amazing miracle she had just experienced over the phone. It had defiantly been Tom's voice. She repeated what Tom had said. Suddenly Gwyn realized that Allie did not seem surprised.

Gwyn stopped her story as the three children came down a back staircase into the kitchen.

Allie was ready with snack bars and drinks for them to take outside with them, so they could do their barn chores and be ready for a weekend visit with grandparents.

While Allie was busy with the children, Gwyn had a moment to absorb her lovely surrounding. The large sitting room must have been added to the house along with the kitchen of all kitchens. Everything around her was beautifully displayed with a lifetime of treasures. The heavily carved oak mantel had a very large antique French clock with matching ornate candle stands. The clock made a peaceful, deep tick - tock sound to add to the homey feel of the room. The bookcases on either side of the fireplace went from floor to ceiling and Gwyn could tell from some of the titles of the books, that she could be entertained thru a lifetime of bad weather days. The furniture was all large and deep, made for the comfort of man, women, or child.

Between the den and kitchen were two pairs of French doors that opened out to a wide covered porch. Here was another pair of wonderful southern rocking chair waiting for someone to come rock in the afternoon sun. A gardener's delight of flower beds and brick walkways had taken generations of dedicated lovers of the land to create. A thick row of late flowering daylilies was holding on to their last yellow blooms of the year. The afternoon wind was trying to blow the yellow petals up into the air to add them to the twirling fall leaves. The masses of flowers were half hiding a white picket fence. The children had left open the gate, which entered small pasture with a huge two-story red barn trimmed in white that must have been standing for many generations. This completed the Norman Rockwell scene in front of Gwyn.

A little puff of a dog appeared from under Gwyn's' chair and waited patiently for Gwyn to invite him up. She tapped the space beside her, and the tiny white and black dog bounced up twice its height to enjoy the friendship of warmth and touch. Gwyn took another sip of the great drink and relaxed. The all over body ache from the long drive was lifting from her.

She is a four mile a day runner and a member of the local gym. She works-out faithfully three times a week. Gwyn is 42 years old, 5'7"and keeps her weigh around 140 lbs. She is graceful in movement and as fit as a Marine wife should be. Gwyn has free time to fill with the girls away at school and Tom gone. She and Tom had always taken pride in staying fit. Gwyn had seen first- hand what too much sugar and fried foods can do to folks in her practice. No medicine can correct what God had given you originally, if you are one of the lucky ones that had been born with a good mind and sound body.

Tom, the name sent her mind back into a tailspin. The flickering hope of love renewed, turned on a happiness in Gwyn what she never though she would feel again. She had to have some answers are go nuts!

Allie was sneaking looks at Gwyn and liked what she saw. She could see the strength and kindness shining through the confusion that the call from Tom had caused. Now the hope of love renewed at the sound of Toms voice had turned a light on in Gwyn's' heart that actually made her shine. Allie asked Gwyn to come join her for some comfort food in the kitchen just as the door- bell ring.

The antique doorbells sharp braying ring made them both jumps. The little dog started a series of sharp pitched yelps, as if he was trying to compete with the sound. Allie told yo-yo to hush, which he totally ignored. The tiny warrior ran for the front door to defend his home and people.

The third wife to except Allies invitation was, Peggy Williams, Jacks' second wife. She was 37 years old and an accomplished criminal attorney from Baltimore, Maryland. Her drive time had been as long as Gwyn's and she was very tired. She hoped this trip would bring her to the end of this roller-coaster ride of emotions called, Jack. Peg wanted a wrap up of these lost months. She had wasted too much time sitting in her apartment with the curtains closed against life, since Jack had lost his. She wanted closure.

Peg was a city girl and did not enjoy what she saw as isolation from the normal busy streets, high rises, and lots of people. After coming off the Interstate, she had been stuck behind a farm tractor pulling a large piece of equipment for several miles. There was no way to pass on such a narrow road. The farmer had finally turned into his driveway and given her a friendly wave as she passed. She had lost her mile count now from zoning out as she had trailed the tractor. She came round a curve and it truly freaked her out, when two large deer were standing in the middle of road. They were blocking her entrance into the driveway that would lead her to, "Willow Farm." She had never seen deer outside of a zoo or park situation and her first though was, do I need to call somebody, but she did not have a clue as to who to call. She beeped her horn and the larger of the two deer turned its' majestic head and for a moment, looked Peggy in the eye. Then the pair jumped into the woods and disappeared into the evening mist.

A light fog was softening the last of the late evening sunlight. It was the end of another beautiful fall day. It was that in between time of the setting of the sun and the start of the moons shine. The deep tunnel of a driveway with its large over hanging trees added an eerie feel to Peggy's already spooked nerves. As she came out of the dark drive and caught her first sight of the large comfortable old home with its welcoming lights shining softly in the windows, her thoughts turned to a hot bath and cozy bed. Suddenly her phone started an odd series of beeps. She answered it as she rolled to a stop in-front of the house. It was Jack.

With the sound of Jacks voice still in her head Peggy slowly made it to Allies front door and pressed the old fashion doorbell. Allie found Peggy standing with a frozen to the spot look, at the front door. Allie and Yo-yo watched as Peggy started shaking from head to toe. Allie called for Gwyn to come and help her. Peggy crumbled to the porch floor. Not in a faint, but because her legs could not hold her up, while her mind was trying to wrap around the sound of Jacks voice, which had reopened the door to her heart.

Allie and Gwyn rushed to help. Peggy's head dropped back as she looked up to Heaven and gave a scream of pure joy. Gwyn and Allie joined in with an amazing mix of tears, laughter, and shouts of giddy happiness. Their most treasured desirer had been returned to these three very blessed hearts.

Gwyn, Allie, and Peggy had started an adventure not of their choosing. There men held the key and tonight they would learn the game they would have to play to have them home again. Allies' children had rounded the house to see what all the shouting was about. They found three of the happiest women on Earth. And as children do, without having to know why, they ran to join in the fun and hugs.

The three women spread their arms to include the children in their joy.

Allies' in-laws came shortly after Peggy's arrival and took their happy grandchildren, just a few miles down the road to their home for a sleep over.

The three wives had nibbled on the wonderful treats Allie had made for their stay. Then they went out to the front porch and sat in the big rocking chairs and gently rocked and let their minds float.

Allie had disappeared back into the house and returned with a bottle of brandy and glasses.

The three women were now linked together in something their husbands had planned. Men they had loved, and thought were lost to them forever. Then with one ring of their phones, their hearts had opened that door, that they thought would never be opened again.

Night birds began calling out to each other. The chill of the evening air made the women stir in their chairs. Allie stood and announced it was time to eat dinner. Yo-yo, who had been sitting in Allies lap, started a little dance around the women's feet to direct them back into the warm house. He was a seven-pound protector that took his job very seriously.

The wife's mission as a team had begun.

Allie had all the fixings of a wonderful feast set out on the counter for them in minutes. Wynn and Peggy had gone upstairs to settle into their rooms.

Allie just wanted to cry. She had been braved for her children, for Edwards parents and now for these two strangers. How could the men who had promised to love and protect them thru life, in front of God and man, put the three of them through such hell. Edward's, letting Allie believe he was gone forever had been such misery. Now, with one phone call Edward was back into her life and heart, as if he had never been gone. And the three husbands were asking the wives to help them with their mission. Twelve months was a long time of pain and tears. Allie hoped the men had an incredibly good explanation.

Allie placed her favorite china out on the kitchen bar. She filled glasses with sweet southern tea over ice. They had to be sober for what was coming in less than an hour. That was the time set by their husbands, to tell them what had been going on to, keep them silent for such a long time. And what part they expected the wives to play in this mission of theirs.'

Allies' heart did a flip at being included again in that special wives' club. She had though she would never be in that grouping again. Edward had always been her one and only since fourth grade. He always made her smile and feel safe and happy. Allie felt that feeling of contentment just thinking about having Edwards arms around her again. She would do whatever it was he asked if it would bring him home to her again.

Peggy had to lay down for a minute. The big soft bed had lots of pillows and the warm covers were perfect for her tired spirit. She had stripped off her travel cloths and taken a quick hot shower. She had her own private bathroom, which Allie had supplied with everything from shampoo, scented soaps, lotions, and lots of soft towels for her guest's comfort. Peg had been to spas that were not stocked as well. Southern hospitality was wonderful. Peg opened her suitcase and dressed in slacks and a navy-blue sweater. She had always been fit and trim. She was a runner and loved to push herself physically. Since Jacks' death or correction, disappearance, she had dropped about fifteen pounds. The weight loose gave her face and body a childlike appearance. Food was not important to her without Jack to share it with. Peggy realized she was very hungry. She ran her fingers thru her short damp hair and headed downstairs.

Gwyn felt as if she was in a dream. Could that have really been her Tom's voice? She could not be still. She kept moving around the room, putting her things in the closet. Putting her make- up in the bathroom. They must have a full bathroom with each bedroom in this big southern house. Everything was so cozy and comfortable. Allie even put books on the bedside table. The bed had lots of pillows with a Lara Ashley spread and matching curtains on the windows. It was all soft and girly. Gwyn loved it. She decided to take a bath later. She wanted to soak in the old claw foot tub in very hot water and hash over all that she was about to hear. She washed her hands and face with a bar of the wonderful smelling soap. Brushed her hair and teeth and headed downstairs for the great food Allie had ready for them. Gwyn had a lighter feeling to her mind and body. The weight of a harsh world was gone from her shoulders. Tom was still alive, and she would do whatever it would take, to bring him back home to herself and their daughters.

CHAPTER 3

Tom, Edward, and Jack had checked into a tourist hotel on the Pakistan side of the border with Afghanistan. They had crossed over the border yesterday, so that they could make the phone calls to their wives with hopes of not being traced. They all had knots in their stomachs over the time that had pasted since they disappeared from the real world. The fear of their wives finding another man to fill in the gaps or if the women would hate their husbands for the deceit and pain the three men had caused them, eat away at any peace, or pleasure the men could get from the first clean room they had been in for over a year. They had taken a three-room suit in the Old Plaza Hotel, on the outer edge of this busy city. Lots of businesspeople and tourist stayed here.

There would be hundreds of out of the country calls being made at any one time. Hopefully, their calls would not be traced back to them or to the girls in the states. Edward had special new cell phones sent along with the equipment installed at his home in Virginia by the undercover

Army technicians, who had secured the house two weeks ago. The calls they made had to be untraceable to keep their families safe.

Edward had been talking to Allie for over a month. It was killing him to have to stay away from home, especially after hearing her voice. He needed to hold her. He loved the way she smelled. She made her own soaps. So, the house and the children all had Allies scent. Edward wanted to go home. They would bring this mission to a close soon if the wives could help them pull off the final ending. The equipment and large television screen that had been set up at, Willow Farm, would give the wives their first look at their husbands since the men disappeared. The husbands would also be able to see their wives. Edward looked in the bathroom mirror for the first time in over a year and almost scared himself. It was way past time for a long hot shower and shave.

Jack and Tom were doing the same. The men were to meet at the restaurant in the hotel for dinner. Edward realized he was very hungry. He stripped out of his dirty cloths and stepped under the hot shower. He decided that food could wait. It was going to take time to clean the sand from his body. He closed his eyes as the hot spray of water hit his face and he thought he could almost smell his sweet Allie.

The girls nibbled on the wonderful food that Allie had made for them. Her sweet southern tea was the greatest. There was not much talking, because all kinds of thoughts were racing wildly in their heads.

Allie had each of them a notebook and pens. So, they could write down anything they might need to talk about later. They knew there would be many questions that needed answers. She turned on the big screen over the mantle and the girls tried to get as comfortable as they could with the nervous tension building like static electricity in the room. They sat on the large sofa next to one another, so the camera would show the wives to their husbands, at the same time they were looking at the men.

A series of numbers that the wives recognized as the same ones that had appeared on their phones came across the large screen over the fireplace. Then there appeared their husbands. The three men that these women loved and always would keep in their hearts. It was such a shock to see them alive and looking strong and very tan in front of them. It took only moments for their voices to start coming thru the sound system. The men all started talking at the same time, but instantly realized that would not work. The girls had to fight back the tears and it was the same with their men. They had been kept apart too long.

Jack spoke first, explaining how he had kidnaped Tom and Edward into this very important mission. And now to end it, they needed the girls to help state side. The girls had each been sent a packet explaining what was needed to be done and why. They had to capture, Abdul Hanson Hemal who was one of the heads of a terrorist group from ISIS.

Then Edward said, "This man is moving four of his wives and three of his children to the United States. They are setting up housekeeping in three Manhattan, N.Y.C. high rise apartments. No one has seen, Abdul Hanson Hemal, in the States. The family is coming in the next few weeks. They will need help setting up school for the kids and the many other things for their new life in the Big Apple. This is one of the big guys that we have been chasing all over the world. If we can catch him, it will stop much of the power play that these wars are about in the Middle East. He has an endless supply of money to run and will come to his women as soon as he can sneak into America. The packets will have the info to set you up with the family, so you will be on the inside and know when he is to show up in the States."

Allie handed the other two wives a large envelope with their name on it. It was very thick and heavy. They would have more research to do even with this books worth of information handed to them.

Tom said, "These are extremely dangerous people with lots of hate for Americans. If you decide to do this mission, you will be stepping into the front line of battle. Abdul's family has asked for a women doctor, a women lawyer and a women decorator and assistant to help them get set up in America. We couldn't think of any three more perfect people for these jobs." Jack said, "So girls what do you think"?

There was dead silent from the three women. They were not thru savoring the moment of seeing their husbands standing, alive and well, before them.

CHAPTER 4

Kevin is six feet tall and has piercing black eyes and a newly shaved head. He is built like a bull. It came from working out twice a day at the prison weights.

It is odd that the prison guards seem to admire prisoners who worked hard on getting bigger and stronger. They were usually the mad dogs that turn on the guards and kill them. The prison Doctor would file the reason for these murders as the prisoner was just suffering from suppressed anxiety and not blame the guard's death on a miss read moment of trust between guard and prisoner. Prison was full of badly made dissensions between people.

On the way to his escape, Kevin snapped the neck of friendly old Tim. Tim was just 3 weeks away from retirement and his first trip to the United States and to Disney World in Florida. He and his wife Annie had saved for years to go to the U.S.

Tim had admired the notoriety of having Kevin in his prison block. Kevin was well-known all-over Europe for the big heists he had pulled off. It was strange that law abiding people could admirer thieves and murders. Annie had made Kevin cookies and treats weekly since he had come to prison. Now Kevin had, in turn, made Annie a widow.

Kevin had been in prison for seven long years. He was serving multiple life sentences for killing three security guards and a secretary at a government lab. He had stolen plans and documents for a military transport radar device. And he had been set up.

Ashley was a tall, exquisite blond American, who spoke perfect French and Arabic. It was the first time Kevin had felt an attachment to anyone. She had used him for the job, taken the documents and then walked away when three soldiers jumped him. As he was led away in handcuffs, he saw Ashley speaking to a man in a suit. They stepped into the back of an official looking black car. Kevin had not heard anything about her involvement in the heist thru-out the trial. It was if she vanished.

He would find her and kill her. No one took seven years of his life and made a patsy out of him and got away with it.

The plans for his," escape," from prison had been made over telephone, computer, and mail. His high-priced attorneys had worked overtime in keeping his rights and privacy safe guarded. The men who wanted him out were in high places. They needed him for a big job. They had not spoken of what the job was yet. They were foolish to think he would stand around and wait on their project, he had many of his own.

The satisfaction Kevin received from killing a kind man like Tim was not much. Kevin had not killed anyone in the time he had been in prison. He had killed many people in his life for money or in protecting himself. Life was not precious to him; it was just a time frame to get thru.

Kevin was very high on the emotion of getting out of this cage he had been trapped in for such a long time. His cell door opened magically at the appointed time. He walked silently down the roll of cells to the door that led to the exercise yard. It opened easily to his push, and he then walked quickly alone the 50-foot-high concrete wall to the guards exit from the yard. There were no shouts or worse, shoots fired at him for being in a locked down area. The heavy metal door opened easily to his pull and no alarms sounded. Kevin was really sweating, and his focus was on one thing, and that was getting out of this Hell hole. He stepped quickly thru the door and into the short hallway with locked doors opening to various secure areas.

Tim had just started down the hall which led to the car park garage to go home for the evening. He was thinking of the pot roast and potatoes Annie was cooking for dinner. He felt rather then heard someone coming quickly up behind him. He gave a surprised smile of recognition at Kevin as he turned around. Tim only had a moment for the flicker of the realization, as to why Kevin would be so close to an outside area. Tim was in the wrong place at the wrong time. Kevin easily snapped his neck and dropped him to the floor. Kevin picked Tim up and put him in the cleaning supply closet. It would be less than an hour before Annie would be calling the prison looking for Tim. The guards would see Tim's car still sitting in it' parking place. And then the clock would be ticking to find out what had happened to Tim in this prison world.

Kevin went to door 3 and stepped into the car park and delivery garage for this freedom side of the prison. It was now 8:30 in the evening, which was inky dark in October. Kevin went to the seventh car on the right side and opened the hatch back of the dark blue Ford Expedition. He grabbed the bag of cloths and stepped toward the front of the car and quickly stripped out of the prison garb and dressed in the jeans, shirt, and perfectly fitting leather jacket. Even the tennis shoes were a comfortable fit for him. The car was an exact match to the prison fleet but tagged differently. No guard would look twice at the car leaving the employee's garage. When Kevin made it to the highway the tags would protect him from being traced for a brief time.

Kevin had to fight to keep his foot light on the gas. He had not been behind the wheel in over eight years. Just seeing the road in front of him without bars or wire in front of his face, gave him an awakening of his spirit. He would kill anyone, including himself, before he would be locked up again.

A plane was waiting for him at a small near-by airport that the attorneys often used coming to see clients at the prison. Kevin was flown to Ireland where he would be met by a jet that would take him to America. The flight attendant handed him a large, sealed packet, as he entered the private plane. The Big Apple was his final destination for the job.

The people who had arranged his escape, wanted him to take out a Middle Eastern terrorist that had been traveling back and forth to the U.S. Kevin would receive the bounty that was on the man's head for doing the killing. Six million was serious money! There was seven-hundred and fifty thousand in hundred-dollar bills in the packet, along with passports and drivers' licenses to match each one. He would do the job. Then he would find and kill Ashley.

CHAPTER 5

The girls had a long sleepless night after seeing their husbands and hearing their voices for the first time in over a year. Their hearts were aching from the stress of it. The shock of losing their husbands had been an awful heart thing to survive. Now finding them alive and well was a recovery they had to think about and wrap their minds around. They had to absorb this wonderful happening into their whole being. They had all agreed it would be the touch that would make true believers out of them. They all needed to be held in their men's arms and have him sleeping beside them at night.

That bond between a man and women could only be filled by the touch of a lovers embrace.

The warmth of a lover's touch could always fill the spirit with strength and power and give balance to their bodies. A single person could not receive the renewing of the spirit without giving back love in a commented relationship of man and women. From the touching of fingertips, to making passionate love, and all the in-between day to day needs, was what kept the hard walk of life bearable. The wives were looking forward to the kiss hello from their husbands, they never wanted to hear goodbye again. There is nothing good about a goodbye.

The men had promised that it would be different as soon as this assignment was over. The three women, like all the other military spouses around the world, had heard that one before.

But now many military wives got the chance of having her lost forever love come back from the grave. And then be asked to participate in the capture of a criminal terrorist.

The smell of a good mug of coffee drifted thru the house and up the stairs. It was early, maybe 6 a.m. and the sun was shining into Peggy's room. She had slept surprisingly well after the evenings shock from Jack. How wonderful to have him back. He was only a half a world away, not until death do, we met. Peggy said aloud to herself, "I will see you and feel you in my arms soon." Life was good. Then she thought, they had never set a date to see one another.

Peggy got up, throw on her robe and went looking for the coffee.

Allie had been the first one up. The big house was so quiet. It was not a lonely quiet, it was a cuddly, friendly quiet. The type of quite that went with the satisfaction you felt when the kids were tiny and safe and asleep in their beds. This house wrapped its arms around you and held you close in your hour of need.

Allie had slept deeply for half the night. Then her thoughts had stirred her mind to half awake.

All she could think of was Edward.

It was hard to believe how the time had flown by since she had opened the front door to a hard knock. It had been late, about 8 in the evening, when two Army officers had stood on her front porch to give her the Armies condolences in the loose of her husband, her children's father, and his parents only son. Ali's spirit had not felt this light since that knock. The tightness that had been in her neck was gone. She would scale any mountain or swim the sea to be back in Edward's arms again. If it required taking down a terrorist to have her best friend and life's partner back home, she would do it.

Gwyn had been sitting on the front porch since a little before five. She had taken a large handmade crocheted coverlet from the closet and wrapped herself up, then sat down in one of the big rockers on the front porch. She needed to be alone with her thoughts. Gwen watched the mornings light creep gently down thru the huge, beautiful, 200-year-old oak tree that stood in the front of the house. She thought the tree limbs must be at least twelve feet around and the tree trunk sixty feet around. It was the size of a mac truck. Oak trees could only grow like this in the south. The trees also had the swirly, soft gray moss hanging from the limbs and it hung down almost touching the ground. The big trees had most likely been here when the northern soldiers passed thru during the civil war. It looked like passed relations to Edward may have planted the beautiful trees in pairs to grace either side of the long drive. Some of the oaks had probably been hit by lighting or just gotten too old, huge, and fallen down because some were missing in the line-up. There were still at least eight big ones starting at the front yard and then placed down the long drive to the road. That was as far as Gwyn could see. The woods had closed in around the last half of the driveway.

The house had been here a long time. Gwyn had read the historical marker beside the front door. The house had been built in 1813 by Edwards great-great-great Grand Father. It was reassuring that a family could love and care for their home for two hundred years. Gwyn felt save and comforted here. She was so glad that she had come on this journey to hear the good news with these fine women and stay in this beautiful place.

The rich smell of good coffee touched her nose. She wanted a cup and then a long, hard run. The men were calling back at noon. Gwyn wanted to make demands of her own. She wanted to talk it over with the girls. She heard the soft mutter of voices as she came in the front door and stated down the hall to the den.

The three wives had spent the morning going over the information that had been sent to Allie for each of them. It was basically the same info in each packet. Then it explained their individual responsibilities to the family.

Allie had heard three times from Edward by phone stressing the importance of getting the women to come to Willow Farm for this meeting. She had then received the three packets of instructions the day before Gwyn and Peggy arrived. The wives were sitting on the sofa in the den awaiting their husband's appearance on the big screen. Each wife had agreed that they wanted a time set for a husband-and-wife reunion. They would travel anywhere in the world to be with their man. That was the only way the women could feel that the men were alive, and the situation was real. They would not take a sucker punch again.

The three women were strong, healthy, and motivated. The feeling of revenge or retaliation had been an emotion that had floated in and out of each of their minds at various times over the past year. But that had been as far as they could take it and stay sane for their families.

It was clear to the wives that they had been brought into the mission because their specialties were needed. It was a task that they would never have dreamed up in a thousand years. Being asked to weave themselves into an Afghan family's daily life to get their lost husbands back. It was a no brainier, than would do whatever it took. And they would have accomplished a since of righting a painful wrong done to their lives.

CHAPTER 6

Toms' heart tried to jump out of his chest when he heard Gwyn's' hello over the phone.

He had so many what ifs in his mind after not commutating with his wife of 23 years for the last thirteen months. Letting her believe he was dead had been the hardest and most heartless thing he had ever done. A few of his what ifs were, had she met another man, or would she hate him for not telling her that he was alive immediately after his disappearance. Would she want to see, hear, and hold him as he wanted her? Gwyn was a South Alabama beauty that any good man would kill to have as his wife. Tom had agreed with his comrades to leave her hanging out there alone, unprotected and hurting. It was a miracle Gwyn had not spit into the phone at the sound of his voice. Tom prayed she would still love him and work with the group on this mission.

Tom is a Marine first and Gwyn had always been a Marines wife first and foremost. The defense of The United States always came first or at least it had in the past.

All three husbands were really rethinking their decision in leaving their families in the dark for such a long time. They had never thought about the mission taking over a year to complete. Time had gotten away from them. They had accomplished much in the 12 months journey they had undertaken in the wilds of the Afghanistan territories. Time had moved at a different pace in this primitive land that resembled Americas, wild west of 1870's. Before they knew it, another month slipped by, and they were still not close enough to the information that they had to have. They were in need of peoples' names and the places used as meetings spots and where the families of the man they were after lived. They needed to know where his money came from. It had taken a little over seven months to even learn the targets name.

Abdul Hanson Hemal was a trader to his country and his people. Because of his blood line and the large army of thuds he commended, money poured into his private bank accounts from all types of people. He wanted to be the World's leader and many evil and greedy people wanted him to succeed to his desire. He was trained by the worst and most evil of humankind. He had been responsible for seeding unrest, which caused brutal civil war among many of Afghanistan's tribes. War was second nature to these people. They had been influenced by countries from all over the world. The people of the back country were farmers by trade. They would grow food for themself and what was left over would be sold or traded for something they needed. They lived simple lives and wanted to be left alone. Because of the demand for opium and pot that grow very well in most areas of their country, these onetime food growers were forced into being drug producers for the landowners. There was now a shortage of food for the people who lived in the outlying farmland. They did not have time for the farming they needed to do for their own families' survival. This type of heavy-handed dictatorship had been going on in this land and the countries surrounding it since the beginning of time. It would be almost impossible to change the mind-set of the majority of the people. They just followed like sheep. They were not even noticing that it was the big bad wolf they were following down the endless trail.

Abdul Hanson Hemal felt very smug to be sending four of his wives, two sons and a daughter to live in the hub of Americas' financial district, New York City. It was a slap in the face of the American laws that were made to protect, The United States, from its enemies. He had flown into America three times in three months. The first time to buy two large spacious apartments.

They were located in an amazing high raise complex in Manhattan. He had purchased the two apartments with the option to buy the third apartment as soon as it became available. The building was across from beautiful Central Park, which had an amazing view this time of year. The first frost had turned the trees into glowing reds, yellows, and golds. It was so hugely different from Abdul's arid, harsh country. He only used cash, so he had to travel a second time with the other half owed the owner of the building. Abdul paid eight and one-half million dollars for the apartments. That was just a drop in the bucket of the percentage of currency he had on hand to use in any way he felt was necessary. He had two jets with pilots and crew. The planes would seat 24 people including bodyguards. Money was no problem for Abdul. People from all over the world sent him money daily. They wanted to see him succeed as world leader. It was because they wanted to buy their way into the right-hand man's spot. They would beg, barrow, steal and kill to supply whatever this man of the devil desired. And then they could ultimately win their hearts desire.

Abdul also had need of a hiding place for three young women he had kidnaped. He had taken them from a village that he had been hired in wipe out and leave no survivors. This tribe had been admired by Afghanistan's peace loving and educated people and many of the like- minded people in the surrounding countries. Abdul and his thuds had lined up and shot all the men, from grandfathers to baby boys. Then they had gathered the women and girls, lined them up in front of the died and dying men. These murderers went down the line of good women and shot the too young, to old, the sick and pregnant first. Then the devils were left with the ones then wanted to play with.

Abdul spotted three beautiful young girls clinging to each other. He took them for himself. He had his men drag the trembling terrified young girls, who were in shock from witnessing all the murders of their families and friends happening around them, into one of the houses. He stripped them of their clothing and raped them in front of his men. The girls were then tied up and left in the house, while Abdul and his group of thuds, with the help of an excavator tractor, made a long shallow grave to cover up the evidence of the brutal murders of a whole village. Generations of families and friends with wonderful hopes and dreams, had come to a horrible end, because of the greed of a few evil devil's helpers. Abdul would leave some of his men at the village for a few days. They would kill any person who might have been away from home or a poor soul just wondering over for a visit. The word would get out fast to the whole country to stay away from the once loving and loved village.

All the surrounding land and the building would be taken over by the greedy murderous thuds that had hired Abdul to kill the villagers. They wanted an undisputed take-over of the oil rich land.

Greed was always the number one monster at play with any kind of manmade wipe out of human life.

Abdul's sexual desires overrode his fear of the evil, greedy people he had made his murderous deal with. He had four wives and twelve children at his home in the out lands of Afghanistan. They lived in a protected fertile valley deep in the snowcapped maintains. Abdul stayed with them for two to three weeks a couple of times during the year. Just long enough to produce new babies for the following season. He wanted his country to be populated with his seed, because he knew he was the chosen one. He saw himself as the smartest, most handsome, and wisest man to have ever come out of the East.

The three girls he was taking were from a special blood line. The tribe and village he had wiped out were known as the wise men of the East. He wanted that blood line to flow through his decedents. Abdul did not understand that kindness, fairness, love, and respect went hand and hand with wisdom.

He knew who these girls were. The births of the three had been celebrated by their parents and countryman. The girls were born into families famous for their contributions in helping the people of Afghanistan. The parents and most of the villagers were educated in medicine, science, and the political policies of the world. Abdul had just wiped out the majority of educated organized voices, that loudly stood for the well-being of his Afghan Countrymen.

Abdul had the girls transported in the back of a covered truck through the dessert and then into the mountains as far as the truck could go. When the road ended a helicopter would take them the last eighty or so miles, as the crow flies, to his farm.

The other wives were not happy. Abdul had sent a message to the farm that three women would be arriving at the farm with-in the next few days. His family, farm workers and guards had heard about the savage slaughter of the brain trust tribe. A traveler hurt on his journey through the mountain pass above the farm had been found by one of the farm workers. The lone man had slipped on the mountain trail and sprained his ankle. He had stayed over-night and told all the news of the happenings back in the cities he had traveled thru.

After hearing the travelers tells the wives were afraid. The women that Abdul was sending to the farm were most likely victims kidnaped from that terrible massacre. He was sending them to the farm to hide them. It would put everyone at the farm in great danger. The other tribes would retaliate against Abdul and all his people if they found him to be involved in the terrible murders. They could not understand why he was doing this.

The three girls arrived three days later. They had been thrown into the back of a covered truck and driven without stopping for seven hours. Their hands were still tied, and a slave cuff and short chain connected the girls to each other's right foot. When the truck stopped, and the men checked on the young prisoners the men at first though they had died. The men knew Abdul would kill them if they could not bring the girls around. They quickly found help with a mid- wife in the small village, where they were refueling the truck. The men would not let the girls be taken from the back of the truck. The mid-wife climbed in and helped each girl drink small sips of water. She had the men bring a large tribal rug made of soft, thick sheep's wool. She then had the men move the girls to the soft rug with several blankets and pillows for each one. The old women spoke harshly to the men and told them the young girls had to have food and rest from what they had been through. She knew the girls had been brutally raped and terribly mistreated. She untied their hands, but there was nothing she could do about the ankle cuffs which were cutting and bruising the tender skin on the girl's feet. She gave each girl more water and a little warm beef broth. She then gave all three children lots of pain killer. The old women started to give them a lethal dose of opium to save them from what was coming. But she knew these men would come back and kill her tribe. She made the girls as comfortable as was possible in the brief time she was given. Then, they were back on their journey for another two-hundred miles of dusty ruff dirt roads.

The girls' youth and the heavy dose of pain killer, the water and warm blankets started to bring them around. They were hurting all over. Rose, the oldest cousin came around first. She managed to sit up in the bumping and climbing truck. It had really helped their bruised bodies to have the thick rug to lie on and the warm blankets and soft pillows. The rug was big and heavy enough to curl up the sides of the truck body and cover a foot of the back of their hard metal ride. The old women had saved their lives with her quick thinking and fast action.

Rose found the jug of water and the cloth sack of fried bread and fruit that the kind old women had, at the last moment, placed inside the back of the truck. She took a swig of the cold spring water and looked at her young cousins. It was so hard to wrap her mind around what had happened to her cousins and all the people she loved. They had just celebrated a wonderful birthday dinner for Lilly, who was only eleven years old. Daisy's twelfth birthday would be in June. Rose was the oldest at fourteen. She would have to be strong for her young cousins. After what they had been thru, she just wanted to cry like a baby for her parents and wished their lives could be put back in place.

The back left tire of the truck climbed over a rock and slowly did a jarring drop and bounce as it made its accent up the steep incline of the path like road they were traveling up. The three girls were being taken to a small air strip at the edge of a mountain range in a desolate area of mountain goats and the Taliban. Rose crawled over to Lilly and dropped sprinkles of the cool water from her fingers on to Lilly's dry cracked lips. She did the same for Daisy. The two young girls stirred. She repeated the drops of water till they both struggled to sit up and thirstily drink from the jug. Rose gave each of them a pancake of fried bread that was wolfed down quickly.

They shared the last of the jug of water and ate the dried fruit. The truck made a grinding lunge at what seemed to be the top of its long bumpy climb and stopped. It was so strange to finally be sitting still and not have the loud engines roar surround them, as the truck struggled to climb what must be a mountain. The drug that the old women had given them had made them almost comatose for many long hours. The girls had no idea how long it had taken them to get to this stopping point. After their long sleep they were all needing to urinate. They took turns squatting in the back corner of the truck by the tail gate. The truck was on an incline sitting at a backward tilt, so the blood-filled urine spilled out the tail gate, down to the bumper and then to the ground. The urine burned the torn and bruised urinary tract of the three young rape victims. Tears filled their eyes for themselves as well as for each other. They were painfully aware of the dangerous position they had been placed. And no one even knew they were still alive.

The men did not come to the back of the truck to check on the girls till the distant rumbling beat of a helicopter traveling toward them made them look to see who was still alive. The first thing the men spotted was the bright red spots on the fresh mountain snow where the blood mixed urine had dripped off the bumper to the ground. They quickly yanked the tarp back with fear of finding their charges dead. They knew this country was not big enough too hid in, if Abdul was not happy. He would slit their throat himself. The men were praying to their God as they looked into the back of the truck. The three girls were staring back at the men with a piercing look from their huge sad eyes. It made the men feel uncomfortable for a moment as they looked at the abused young girls. The terrible evil they had helped comment on this peaceful tribe of Afghanistan had become a weekly routine. It was the first time in the men's lives that they looked inside themselves, even for a moment, to question the moral issue of the right and wrong of what happened to these girls and their tribe.

Abdul's helicopter made its noisy landing on the natural rock pad for the final leg of the girls' journey to Abdul's farm encampment. The helicopter was the quickest and safest way in or out of Abdul's farm. He had been given the land for doing varied jobs for different drug lords. It was his as long as he was willing to fight for its ownership. He had killed off the past tribe that had worked the opium and marijuana fields in the rich fertile soil of a thousand plus acre valley, deep in these harsh mountains that bordered Pakistan.

Abdul's oldest wife, Jaya met the helicopter with three of the guards. She had expected three grown hostile women, not the three pitiful children that were handed over to her care. The poor girls were weak from the shock of what they had witnessed and the pain of being raped. Jaya told the guard's, "Remove the leg chains now." Then, ordered the men to carry the hurting girls gently up the path and into a low built stone hut. It was separate from the over crowed housing of the other wives and their children. Jaya ordered a fire built in the stone oven of the small one room structure on this cold fall afternoon. Jaya called for the other women to come and help. They gently undressed and bathed the three girls and dressed them in the heavy clothing that the women made from the wool gathered from their herd of sheep. Jaya had more blankets and bedding made up for the girls. When they were clean, dressed and made comfortable with a small dose of opium. The women spooned thick mutton soup to each girl.

Jaya asked their names and when they told her, she instantly knew who Lilly, Daisy and Rose were and why Abdul had kidnaped them. These three girls were known all over Afghanistan and the surrounding countries. Their mothers were sisters and had married men of the same tribe.

These people were famous, outstanding Statesmen of Afghanistan. The women were outspoken leaders in women right and pushers for educating the children of Afghanistan, both boys and girls. Abdul would never get away with this monstrous deed.

Jaya washed and brushed the girl's thick shining black hair and then bradded it loosely for a comfortable sleep. One of the other women brought in a tray of goats' cheese and fried bread, if the girls became hungry during the evening. Jaya told them to rest and that she would be back to check on them later. The pain killer was already working on the three. They could hardly keep their eyes open. As Jaya closed the door, so closed the three pairs of sad eyes.

CHAPTER 7

Rose, Lilly, and Daisy's mothers were sisters. They had always felt so blessed to have spent their lives together. The three sisters had been promised at an early age to three young man of the same tribe close to their parent's home. Certain men in this educated tribe were called the wise men or brain trust of Afghanistan. They oversaw making the laws for general tribal life. Their village was where court was held if the law breakers were in their region. Afghanistan is a large country, and these three husbands were appointed to travel and hold court in small and large cities all over the country. The three wives of these judges, the sisters, were also well educated and respected by their kinsman and country. The three wives knew how special it was for three of them to live and raise their children in what they thought to be a safe spot, in a country that stayed at war.

The girls had been the only children the sisters and their husbands wanted to have. They had named each child after the mothers' favorite flower and the fathers were delighted.

The cousins had started their education as soon as they were old enough to read. The village had a school for the boys and a separate school for the girls. Both were taught the same course of studies and were even brought together to be evaluated at the end of each semester. The best students for the year were rewarded with a trip to some historical spot in the Easter part of the world. These students were the hopeful leaders needed to make a difference in Afghanistan. This Tribe wanted to end the third world way of life of its' people.

The three young cousins had become world travelers at an early age. Their parents had taken them to see London, Paris and of course, traveled all over America. The girls and their mothers had flown to, New York City, as a family and spent two weeks each year at a beautiful hotel. The happy group shopped and visited the wonderful museums that seemed to be everywhere in the city. The girls had enjoyed the Broadway plays and going for walks in the amazing parks and busy streets with their wonderful mothers. The girls had been raised to be shining stars. They understood the meaning of being treated special and being genuinely loved. They would rise from this horrible circumstance. That evil had created to destroy good people. They owed their parents for the strength of right they felt in this primitive world they had been thrown into. They would survive and prevail.

The three small girls went to sleep holding hands and laying close to each other in the cold hut. They were clinging to the only piece of the past left to them in the upside-down world they were now in. They felt blessed to have each other. Their bedding was a medium size thick rug over a packed and swept dirt floor. They had four or five heavy woolen blankets for cover from the mountain cold. They were quickly deep asleep.

By morning, the fire had burned down low in the stone stove. There was a small stack of wood against the wall by the door. The icy morning air and pale light shining thru a small window awoke Rose. She crawled out from her warm spot under the blankets to add wood to the dying fire. She could see her breath in the frosty air. The girl's bathroom was a pot in the corner. A small table with one stool was in the middle of the room.

There was a small one pane window that actually opened to let the smoke and other odors out and fresh air in. Rose tried to open the big heavy plank door, but it would not budge. Her cousins had not stirred yet from their deep drug induced sleep. Rose worked on the fire and had it blazing in no time. She went to the pot and relieved herself. It did not hurt her so bad this time. She was most worried about Lilly. She was the youngest and smallest of the three girls. That horrible man had raped little Lilly first. He had been the most aggressive with the smallest of them. Lilly had been passing lots of blood. The women had packed soft rags into her to hopefully stop the bleeding.

Rose splashed her face with the chilly water she found in a bowl on the table. There was also a wonderful smelling bar of soap in a small dish. It felt good to wash her hands and face. She took the water jug and left-over cheese and bread from last night and went back to her cousins. Rose crawled in between her cousins and spoke in a whisper soft voice to wake up. Daisy stirred and slowly sat up. Lilly just whimpered and half rolled over. Rose told Daisy to take a sip of water. She thirstily drinks from the small jug. The two girls eat some of the creamy goats' cheese with the usual fried bread.

Then it was Daisy's turn to crawl out from under there warm nest and refreshed herself on the slop pot. She then splashed the icy water on her face and washed her hands in the large bowl with the same water. Daisy did a twirl around once overlook of their little twelve by twelve room. She was a beautiful young girl with the promise of great beauty. Her face had the features of a perfectly chassed marble statue shaped by Michael Anglo's love for beauty. Daisy's body was always graceful in its graceful movements. Her cloths always seemed to fit and look the best of the three girls. Her beauty also came from the inside. Daisy was kind and compassionate of everyone she met. She was quite a good listener and a quick learner. She was always mulling over the things her parents and their friends talked about after a good evening meal together. At twelve Daisy knew about her country's politics. The wrongs and the rights, the good and the bad, of how Afghanistan was run. She had just lived thru the worst.

Just at that moment the scraping sound of the slide bolt on the outside of the heavy door sent Daisy running to join her cousins. Jaya stepped in with a tray of breakfast foods for the girls. She was very relieved to find two of them setting up and looking brighter eyed then yesterday.

The smaller child seemed to still be sleeping. Another women stepped in carrying two more chairs for the little table.

Jaya asked the girls to come to the table and eat. Daisy tried to gently shake Lilly awake, but she stirred, tried to set up, moaned and slowly laid back down. Jaya told the girls to leave Lilly resting and come to the table. They hesitated for a moment, not wanting to leave Lilly. Jaya came and squatted down in front of the girls and told them Lilly would be ok. She was just smaller and had been give more pain killer then Rose and Daisy because of her heavy bleeding. Jaya said she was going to feed and clean Lilly up where she lay, she did not want her to move much which might start the bleeding again. Jaya held out her hands to the worried girls and smiled at them. Rose's thick curly hair had escaped most of the bradding that Jaya had fixed the night before. It framed a halo around beautiful face of ivory skin and large almond shaped black eyes. All three girls were small framed and graceful of movement and would defiantly be outstanding beauties. After what they had seen and the horrible things that had been done to them, they could still reach out and take a stranger's hand in trust. They both took a hand and Jaya gently helped them out from under the covers. Jaya made a silent vow to God that she would do her best to protect these precious girls. They had already won her heart.

The girls sat at the table as the other women poured them a glass of fresh creamy milk. The women had prepared the girls quit a feast. There was tender lamb cut in tiny bit size pieces, soft scrambled eggs, dried fruits, and soft baked bread with fresh butter and jelly. The two girls eat hungrily.

As they were finishing a loud knock sounded at the door. One of the other women whose name was Sara opened the door a crack, then opened it wide for two men to carry in a large copper bathtub. It was placed near the fire. They also brought in a tri fold screen to give the bather privacy. The men started bringing in steaming buckets of water to fill the tub. After several tripes the tub was half full of water and the men left. Jaya helped Lilly remove her cloths under the blankets and wrap up in a large soft cloth. Then she helped Lilly come out from under the blankets and slowly walk to the tub. She explained that it would help Lilly's soreness to soak in the hot water. Jaya had removed the rag packing while Lilly was still lying down. The bleeding seemed to have stopped. Lilly relieved herself to the little pot that had been cleaned by Sara. Lilly was then helped into the comfortable warm tub of water. Sara poured a wonderful smelling mixture of herbs and stirred it into the bath water. The mix had been grown and dried from there kitchen herb garden. Jaya had also added the wild herbs that grew in the valley and along the mountain side. The aroma of the mixture was the fragrance of mountain air in the late spring. Lilly was given a fresh bar of soap and a soft hand-woven washcloth. She washed herself all over. Then Jaya loosen her hair from the brad and gently washed Lilly's beautiful long black hair. It seemed to almost glow with a deep luster shine. It was trying to curl from being bradded the night before, but after the washing and brushing it would be silky and straight. The women added more hot water and more herbs. The steam from the hot water and the refreshing smell of the herb mixture seemed to relax the two women and the three girls. The air in the hut almost had a flavor to it. Jaya took deep breaths and told the girls to do the same.

Jaya helped Lilly out of the tub and wrapped her in a large clean towel and her hair in a head wrap. Then Jaya told her to sit at the table with her cousins. The three girls reached for each other's hand with a loving smile. As their hands clasped, a bright warm beam of yellow light from the sun shot thru the small window and seemed to explode around the three young girls. It took Jaya and Sara's breath away. Then dropped to their knees and said a pray for themselves and the girls. Jaya and Sara knew they were blessed to have had the girls placed in their care.

And they made God a promise to protect them. The tub was drained and refilled for Rose and then the same for Daisy. They had a wonderful soak.

The large rug the girls had been given, by the old women, to protect them on their trip in the back of the truck, had for some reason been rolled up and sent on the helicopter with them. Jaya and Sara had cleaned and dried it in the sun, and it was placed on top of two older rugs that covered the dirt floor from wall to wall.

The men built three single beds from olive branches and ruff cut lumber. They had cut the lumber from the small trees that grow on the sides of the mountains around them. The trees supplied them with all their building needs as well as the ever-important firewood.

The girls' room was taking on a whimsical look. The men put the heavy thick, soft wool rugs on the beds and Sara added blankets and two large, overstuffed pillows for each bed. The girls would be amazingly comfortable tonight. It was late afternoon by the time the room was set up and they all needed a rest. The men went back to their regular jobs of sheep herding and checking on the farm chores. The men had become enamored with the young girls and passed the word to the workers and guards up on the mountain sides that they thought the beautiful, sweet girls were Angels from God.

It had been four months since Abdul had been to the farm. His four wives were proudly waiting for his blessings on the latest babies born into the tribe.

Abdul would have a private meeting with each woman and count the days from conception to delivery. If there was any questionable length of days from when he was home or not home, Abdul would have the women and child put to death and thrown out in the mountains for the wild animals to eat. It had always been an excuse used by men to get rid of women who were old or worrisome.

It also put the eye of question on any other child that women had produced. Most times, these children were sold into the slave trade. So, each wife was incredibly careful to not becoming attracted to any of the men around this lonely farm outpost.

Of his tribe, Abdul trusted his first and oldest wife the most. He tried to think how long they had been as one. Jaya had been given to him as a gift when he turned seventeen. Jaya must have been twelve. Abdul was forty-three now, so she was in her late thirties. He would send her with the three girls to New York. He would also send their two young sons and two-year-old daughter.

It had gotten to crowded at the farm. He would either have to build more houses or get rid of some of the women. They were still good workers. The farm was run smoothly. But that was really Jaya 's doing. He would have to turn the running of the farm over to one of the men when Jaya moved to New York.

Abdul was also worried about the security in the remote spot. He had to many enemies that wanted him dead. They believed an eye for an eye in his country. Moving some of his family to New York would protect his tribe from being wiped out. He hoped the three girls were with his seed. If they were not, he would be with them soon in America. It would be good to have them where medical help was so easily available. They were not built for the tough life in the mountains. If it had not been for Jaya's natural mid-wife abilities, some of the other wives and children most likely would have died.

Abdul's and Jaya's four oldest sons were already a part of his army. Jaya had skipped producing children for about five years after their fourth son was born. Abdul had been more interested in the two young twin sisters he had been given. Their drug lord father needed Abdul's protection for his shipments of opium from his farm. Both women had produced him four children each. Abdul would keep those children at the farm. They were from generations of farming families and just naturally seemed to know what to do with the crops and animals. Abdul had been given twenty black angelus heifers and a bull by the United States as a farm project. The U.S. had shipped them to Afghanistan and then the American Army had helicoptered the animals to his farm. The cows as well as the herd of hundreds of sheep and goats were free range. The cows had done very well on the mountain grasses. The herd was growing. Abdul hoped the Americans would bring him more free cattle.

CHAPTER 8

The calls came Monday morning from the State Department to Gwyn, Peggy, and Allie 's cell phones. They were asked to fly to N.Y. City for an interview with the lawyer for a foreign family. The family would pay their flights and stay. The wives would be expected in N.Y.C. by Thursday.

It had been an amazing weekend. Gwyn, Peggy, and Allie had bonded in their commitment to helping apprehend this evil man and get their families life back.

They had an early breakfast Monday morning together. Allie had made fresh biscuits with homemade strawberry jam, fresh eggs from the farm's chickens and thick slices of smoked bacon. Gwyn and Peg drove away with half a dozen cookies and biscuits with ham and cheese for snacks on their drive and of course a large mug of coffee to go. They had come away from Allie's home a few pounds heavier, but with much lighter hearts.

The wives had been briefed on the lives that Abdul's families lived. They had a tough time comparing their love for their husbands and family to the breeding farm relationship Abdul had with numerous wives and children that he was never around to love and raise. It had not taken the wives long to see the differentness between their lucky lives as Americans and the hard lives of these women under Abdul's dictatorship.

It was clear that the Gwyn, Peggy, and Allie were expected to accomplish an especially important task that in their wildest dreams they would never have though up would never have thought up. The plan their husbands developed in there long stay in the hostile land of the Taliban, was the key to the end of their wife's heartbreak. The three American women were strong, healthy, and motived. The feeling of revenge, retaliation or just hurting the people that had screwed up their lives, had been floating around in each of their minds for a year. That had been as far as they could take it and stay sane.

Those aggressive feelings would keep them on the path to complete this mission and get their husband's home.

CHAPTER 9

Jaya had been trapped in this lost desolate valley for over twenty years. When she was just twelve years old the father, she had never really known had come into the low mud block over crowded structure she and her mother shared with five other wives and their children. The only friend Jaya and her mother had was each other.

Too early one morning, Jaya's father had stepped into the door of the dorm type living quarters and pointed at her mother and said, "come." She was not one of his favorites. She had only miscarriages since the birth of Jaya. He had not been with her in ten months. Jaya knew not to speak or responded in any way to what was happening. Just a look would get you slapped hard. This man had slapped Jaya so hard the last time he had come into the building to call one of the wives, that she sailed across the room and hit the stone wall. This time she squatted in the corner by their bed rolls with down cast eyes. The tears spilled down her face from fear for her mother.

Jaya start the morning chores of rolling up their sleeping blankets and putting their hairbrush and sleep shirts in a small basket her mother had made for them. The women and children were just finishing their breakfast of fried bread that was stuffed with squash and wild onions. Jaya slipped a pocket bread into their basket for her mother.

The children went out to the fields to weed the opium, marijuana, or vegetable plants. The women cleaned up their dorm style living quarters and started the evening meal before joining them. If you wanted a mid-day meal you saved part of your breakfast to eat later. Everyone in the house of Lais Mahir was thin, accept Mahir. He was overweight and he kept his guards fit. They always eat before the women and children, who eat what food was left. He was a cruel and greedy man.

Jaya was heading out the door just as Mahir came back into the cooking area. He pointed at Jaya and said come. Jaya had never been acknowledged by her father before and she froze in place.

It was the first time Mahir had really looked at his daughter. She was small and delicate like her mother. He should have known better then to take as a wife someone built like that. They were never good breeders. He had only this small useless girl to show for at least ten years of upkeep. He was glad to get rid of both mother and daughter.

Mahir told the women to bath and dress Jaya. She would be leaving shortly. Mahir did not share with the women his plans for the child. He had made a deal with another drug lord to give him Jaya in exchange for his drug caravans safe travel. This man was going to give her to his son for a wife or to use as a servant. The seventeen-year-old son Abdul could decide.

The girl would be sold into the slave trade. Mahir was also getting rid of her useless mother. He had paid out money four times to the doctors to help her deliver still born sons. He would waste no more food, living space or money on the two women.

Jaya did not understand what was happening. She just did what she was told. She was ruffly scrubbed from head to toe as she stood in a large metal foot tub. Her long black hair was washed and perfumed, then brushed till it was soft and shining. Charcoal was rubbed with fingertips around her large brown eyes. Jaya's father sent a beautiful dress and robe of deep purple with gold trim as her bridal gown. Her veil was a dark purple netting with heavy gold tassels around the edge to weigh it down and keep her face covered. She even had small slippers to match. Jaya had seen many of her half-sisters dressed like this and she had never seen them again.

Where was her mother? Jaya started shaking all over from the fear of the unknown. The women who were dressing Jaya felt a slight moment of pity for the small girl. The women told Jaya in short graphic terms what was going to happen to her. And that Jaya should be grateful to move to a house where she would have her own babies. Unless she was no good like her useless mother.

Jaya was made to drink a drugged concoction that tasted terrible. At this point she did not care anymore. She was small and under feed, so the drug completely knocked her out. Her life and mother became a distant blur floating around in her mind. The sounds and movements around her were wrapped up in a strange shadowy haze. She only weighed about seventy pounds. The man that came for her though he was coming for a woman, not a sleeping child. He never asked questions, just did what he was told. He had to carry the sleeping child to the truck, they had given her to much opium, and she was out. Another women was already loaded in the back of his truck. She was being sent to work in the markets of Kandahar. She was also heavily drugged. He would have a peaceful drive today.

Jaya and her mother never knew that they had shared this last ride together. The mother had been dressed in the traditional black dress, down to the black slippers on her feet. She would be worked in the market in the out skirts of Kandahar till she died of hunger or the cold. Jaya did not know when her mother was unloaded from the truck. She was never awake enough to know that they had shared a blanket and that they had laid beside each other for the last time.

Jaya was still only half awake then the truck came to a halt. She was dragged out of the back of the truck by her foot, which was the easiest put of her for the man delivering her to reach. She was having a tough time standing up after the drugs and the four-hour bumping ride in the back of a swaying truck.

Seventeen-year-old Abdul took the first women he had ever been with, dragged her by the arm into a small block building at the edge of his fathers hundred-acre marijuana field. He through her on the dirt floor and raped her once, then decided to do it again. Jaya was sobbing for relief as he turned and walked out. It was good that she was still numb from the drug the women had given her this morning or she would have died from the experience.

One of the women from Abdul's fathers house came to care for Jaya and found her lying in the middle of the room crying and bloody from the brutal treatment. She was taken to the women's quarters, which was ten times better than her father's house. She was gently placed on thick wool rugs in an area in-closed with heavy curtains. For the second time in a day, Jaya was bathed, and her torn gown was taken away for cleaning and repair. She had survived.

Jaya produced Abdul four sons by the time she was eighteen. Abdul was a rising star in the terrorism movement in the Middle East. Safety was always a big concern for the families of terrorist. He moved his growing tribe out to the farm in the mountains. Abdul had added three more wives. First came Sara and then the two sisters Moire and Asia. Abdul stayed busy entertaining himself with the new women on his random short visits to the farm, much to Jaya's relieve. The three women produce him several sons and daughters. He then started wanting to be with Jaya again. She had been a very productive wife. She soon produced two more sons and then a beautiful little girl.

Abdul also realized Jaya 's importance to the farm. She was an excellent manager of people and the farm. Jaya had seen to the planting of apple, fig, and olive orchards all along the edge of the valley. The trees were now fifteen years old and produced enough for the household and to sale at the markets. They used the produce as a cover for the opium and marijuana shipments. So, he decided to leave her to manage the improvements on the farm instead of looking after babies. She was helping in make him a rich man.

Jaya stood by the door to the kitchen in the afternoon sun. The kitchen was part of the large building that housed Abdul's private apartment that had a large bathroom with a wonderful shower and a beautiful marble tub thanks to the engineering efforts of the United States Army. The farm had been given the best and largest generators that the U.S. could buy. The main complex had two bathrooms with a large shower room. When Abdul was gone the wives took turns using his wonderful tub. Abdul made short visits to check on the farm and the wives every few months. He had not come in over three months.

All the wives were content with the long absences of their dictator. Jaya watched as the three flowers came back from the fields. The young women had gotten into the daily routine of farm work. They were incredibly good with the care of young sheep. They also helped with the many hours of the weeding of the opium fields and vegetable gardens. They seemed to have adjusted to the harsh conditions and isolation of mountain life. It had also been long enough to know that none of the three were pregnant. Jaya was relieved. Abdul would not be happy. Jaya had prayed that something would happen to save the three special girls from a life of babies and hardship.

Jaya was about to get an answer to her pray that she would never have imagined.

Abdul sent the message by helicopter the next morning. Jaya was told to take her two boys and daughter along with the three flowers and leave in the helicopter the next morning. They would be flying to the airport in Kandahar to meet Abdul's jet, which would be taking them to New York City in America. They would have a layover in London, England to get their documents pushed thru.

Early the next morning, Jaya took her three children into Abdul's bathroom washed them from head to toe and dressed them in their best cloths. She had told the girls to be ready to leave by sunrise. She and the girls dressed in the traditional long black dress and head scarf. The pilots and co-pilot helped them climb aboard and they were off.

Jaya could not believe it. She had never thought about her life making such a change. She had never dreamed of being anywhere but the farm. She had no idea what Abdul had planned for any of them beyond the flight. They arrived in Kandahar in two hours. A large black car met them at the helicopter landing pad. They were then whisked away to a small private airport where Abdul's beautiful jet sat, engines warmed up, waiting to take them to a different world.

CHAPTER 10

Gwyn made the drive home to Alabama much faster than the road trip going to Virginia. The nagging unanswered questions that had been hanging heavily around her neck like a boat anchor was gone. She had a mission to do, and she would see Tom soon. Life is good again!

Gwyn unloaded her suitcases from the car. It was great to be back in her wonderful home. She started her laundry first thing so she could re-pack the suitcase again for her tripe to N.Y.C. She had been away from home for a little over two weeks. She glanced at the clock and the glowing numbers read six twenty-five p.m. She poured a glass of her favorite wine and headed to her big tub to start the hot water flowing. Gwyn heard her cell phone ringing. She had left it on top the washing machine when she was unpacking her suitcase. She made a mad dash for the phone and snatched it up on the fifth ring. Tom's deep voice said, "Hi baby." The sound of his voice filled her with a wonderful allover desirer. Gwyn flopped down in Tom's big chair in the den and listen to the sound of his deep amazing voice. At first, they talked about her drive, the girls and family. She told him about settling the twins back into college for their second year. And how much they loved the wonderful campus of Auburn University and the "War Eagle," football. The girls were safe living with each other, and they both lived a healthy lifestyle. Gwyn and Tom were lucky to have identical twins who were like two peas in a pod.

Suddenly Tom said, "I love you, Gwyn. I am so sorry about how this mission happened and how long I have kept you hanging. Please forgive me."

Gwyn though about it for a moment with tears filling her eyes. Then she said, "It has been a horrible experience. It let me know how precious you are to me and that I will love you always."

Tom said, "Edward and Jack and I are coming to see all of you with in the next seven to ten days. It will be in New York City. We have not arranged it yet. We still must keep everything under wraps. They talked till the dark night shadows were deep in the house in Alabama and the sun was bright and shining in Tom's hotel room. They said good night. Gwyn went to their bedroom, which did not seem so lonely anymore. She decided to forget the bath. She slipped out of her cloths, pulled back the covers and crawled into the big bed. Then she thought what number he called me from. She turned her phone back on and did the caller search. There was no phone number or evidence that she had received a call. Just as she slipped into sleep, Gwyn 's thoughts slipped into the dream world of nightmares. Her sleep was restless and haunting. She dreamed she was running thru a dark curving wooded trail desperately calling her girls. She would almost catch a glimpse of them as they rounded the bend in the ever-curving narrow path. Gwyn was breathing hard as her mind ran to find her children. As she rounded the curve in her imaginary dream race, there stood Tom holding hands with Amiee and Mazie. They were all calling for her to join them. And she did. Gwyn awoke with the bright, warm Alabama sun shining thru the windows. It was inviting her to come out and take a run. So, she did.

Gwyn made morning calls to her Mom and other family members and explained about the short-term job she was taking in New York City, and that she would only be home a few days. She was extending her leave from work too, "I don't know when I will be back," was her answer with family as well as her work. The family gathered at her brother's house for dinner that evening, and everyone was happy to see color in Gwyn's cheeks and excitement in her eyes again. Her Mom would drive Gwyn to the airport on Thursday morning and stay at her house till she returned. So, the plan was under way.

Thursday came with Gwyn, Peggy and Allie arriving in N.Y.C. with-in two hours of each other. The trio quickly settled into their amazing hotel rooms. Then, they went to meet with a representative from Abdul's family at the hotel restaurant at six o'clock that evening. It was now just three in the afternoon. The wives decided to walk down the street and look around. After walking less than two blocks from the hotel the three stopped in front of the shop windows of an amazing looking store. It was a dress and every woman's favorite, beautiful shoes shop. They could not resist going into the store. Peg bought beautiful brown leather knee height boots that looked amazing. Allie purchased slacks and two heavy cable knit sweaters in lime green and deep blue. Gwyn bought two pairs of shoes. One the usual brown leather loafer except these were made from alligator and had gold tassels on the top. The other pair of shoes were bright red, pointed toe high heels to match a deep red low-cut dress. She was planning her first date with Tom. Gwyn wanted to knock his socks off. It was a short and awfully expensive first shopping trip together, and it was only day one.

They were staying in one of the trendy hotels just off Broadway. There was plenty of shops, restaurants, and bakeries on both sides of the street. The theaters started just two blocks over from their hotel. N.Y.C. was its own country. You had everything that you could dream up all around you. Of course, the outside world provided everything for all the city dwellers. They were not self-maintained in their world of concrete and people.

The wives hurried up to their rooms to drop off their purchases and freshened up before meeting with the family's attorney. At five forty-five the wives gathered in the hotel lobby relaxed from their shopping adventure and from the realization that they had quickly become best friends. They were also people watchers and comparing their thoughts on different people walking into the lobby.

Just before six o'clock a nervous looking young man walked into the lobby. The wives were sitting on a long comfortable leather sofa in the side reception area of the lobby. They wanted to see the man they were to start their mission with before he saw them.

Moser Hasan Ahtan had lived in New York City for seventeen years. He had been sent to America at eleven to live and work for relatives. He had been granted political asylum because his family was murdered in Iran. He had been given all the food stamps, free education, and housing thru out his life that America always hands out to the needy. His family sponsors also received money monthly until Moser was eighteen. He graduated with a free education from Harvard in political science and law. Moser now worked full time, thanks to his expensive education from America's taxpayers, in a beautiful office in Manhattan. He was also on 24-hour call for Afghanistan terrorist, Abdul Hanson Hemal.

Moser loved the busy world of N.Y.C. He had a beautiful American wife and daughter of Irish decent. Both his girls were fiery red heads. They lived in a large plash Fifth Ave apartment and his daughter went to an expensive private school. Abdul had not been active in Moser's life other than the usual paperwork, until the last three months. He was now constantly on call for this cousin, Abdul. His wife wanted to have Abdul for dinner and treat him as she treated all her happy hardworking American relatives. Moser did not want this murderous man in his house.

The apartment purchase had been tricky. The purchase had to be put in Abdul's wife Jaya's name. Abdul was on the no entrance terrorist list to America. So of course, he could not buy property in the States. The owner of the apartment complex was from Syria and knew all about Abdul and his life expectancy. He required him to pay for the two apartments separately and in cash and to put seven years of property tax and building maintenance fees in escrow. Money was no object to Abdul, it flowed to him like rain from the Gods or the devil. So, Moser opened the housing allowance and escrow accounts in the First Nation Bank on the corner just up the street from the apartments. The bank was incredibly happy with the large amount of money deposited into three separate accounts all in Jaya's name. There was also a fourth account opened to cover all the expenses of the setting up of the family's home. It was the account Allie would be using to buy the home furnishings for the family.

The meeting with Moser had gone without a hitch. He basically wanted to turn the whole situation over to Allie, Gwyn, and Peggy. Moser took them to dinner in the hotel restaurant and talked over the legal aspects of Allie signing the checks and sending a copy of the checks and receipts of purchases to Moser's secretary. He told them that money was no object. That Jaya and the rest of the family were expected in the city with in the next ten days to two weeks. So, he needed the women to start immediately to furnish the house as quickly as possible. They talked about the two apartments the family would be living in and the third one the guards and staff would be sharing. Moser ask Peggy and Gwyn if they could help Allie with the decorating of the apartments. That he would pay all of them handsomely for their over time. The women accepted his very generous offer and agreed to meet him at the apartment building in the morning at eight o'clock.

Moser enjoyed his meal and the time spent with the nice capable women. He felt so satisfied to have this job managed quickly. He could now put this complicated assignment of Abdul's on the back burner. Moser wanted to take a holiday to Disney World in Florida with his wife and daughter that was planned for next week. He felt he would be able to leave everything in these women's hands. So, he turned the fox lose in the hen house.

Gwyn's job did not start until the family arrived, so she was excited to work for Allie on the buying of beautiful things for the apartment. She had to wait to examine the children and see their past shot and health records. There would be the setting up of dentist appointments as will. Gwyn only had the ages and boy and girl. Moser had no other information on the family. He knew nothing about the women or wives that Gwyn would look after.

Peggy started at eight o'clock Friday morning trying to work out the details on the visas and stay permits for the seven-member family. She was also setting up language classes for the women and had to find a school for the children. But in N.Y.C. everyone stops doing legal business by noon on Friday. So, Peg was on the phone to Gwyn and Allie to ask if they needed help and wanted to meet for lunch.

Allie and Gwyn had already ordered the complete kitchen set up from pots and pans to mixers, blenders, and linens. The kitchen had been set up with the biggest and best refrigerator, a six- burner gas stove with two ovens. It had the state-of-the-art large dishwasher and ice maker. Allie and

Gwyn had been studying the instruction manuals so they would be ready to explain how everything worked. Allie had never supplied complete packages before without meeting and understanding the owners likes and dislikes. She and Gwyn had talked it over and decided all the necessities that they could think of would be in place when the family arrived. Then Allie and the wives could pick out colors and accent pieces for the rooms. Any sofa or chair could be exchanged.

The only information Allie had to go no was the estimated age of the children and no info on the wives. Allie had only decorated for American families or couples. So, she guessed she would go with a fun theme of Adirondack Mountain style with snowshoes and fishing signs on the walls for art and bunk beds with double on the bottom and single on the top. The boys had two large bedrooms that was joined by a full bathroom with a large shower and separate bathtub in between the rooms. The boys were thought to be around six and eight and the little girl was supposed to be about four. Allie and Gwyn were excited to be shopping for toys to fill the shelves and toy closet of the children's rooms. The little girl would get a princess's theme for her room with a beautiful double bed with frills and of course several beautiful baby dolls.

Allie would work out the cloths shopping when they met and saw what was needed. She would be their personal shopper until they felt comfortable doing it themselves.

The girls joined Peggy for lunch at a trendy looking restaurant less than a block from the apartments. They were served wonderful fresh salads and baked salmon with crab meat stuffing. It was served in small portions with great taste. As they eat, they talked about the jobs in front of them. They agreed not to forget the real reason they were involved with this job. But they were having fun, especially with an unlimited budget, getting things ready for the family.

CHAPTER 11

Abdul had checked out the apartments and was still not happy with the security. It was adequate for his women and children when he was not in the building. When he was in the city, he wanted total lock down capabilities. Then the women arrived, three of Abdul's guards would stay with them to protect the women as well as drive them around the city. He would replace the men with three new guards every two months. That way no one became attached to the women. Abdul encouraged his men to keep an eye on one another. He would reward the tattle teller and kill the one told on. Abdul's men walked an exceptionally fine line. Only his most trusted guards traveled with him or stayed around his women. Abdul's men would kill without hesitation to protect Abdul or to carry out his orders.

If they did not, Abdul would kill them and their families. The secret of being a dictator was keeping complete control, with the fear of what if, over the people that you surrounded yourself with. Abdul held a proverbial knife at their throat, which was the life of their families.

Abdul was a handsome man in a hard aggressive bad boy way. He was six feet tall with his boots on. His skin had a golden bronze glow from playing golf all over the world. His thick black wavy hair had a scattering of silver thru it that he thought gave a halo effect to his face. Abdul kept his thick beard neatly trimmed. He enjoyed having beautiful women come to his penthouse of whatever country he was staying in to trim his hair and beard and do his nails. He loved the wonderful lifestyle access power and money could get you. His large brown eyes were deep and dark in color. No one could tell what he was thinking. Abdul always kept a straight face, it had a look of being satisfied, weather he was with beautiful women or at a massacre the look was always the same. The ladies were all over him with that Omar Sharif look of the late and famous actor. Who would not fall for the man and his money, if the women looking, did not find out about his black heart and murderous ways? He partied and played golf with the other rich bad boys of the Middle East. Abdul and some of his co-harts had been in Beverly Hills, California for a week. The men had surrounded themselves with beautiful young starlets when they were off the golf course. Life was good for these evil men. There was always someone or a group or even a country that needed their services. They were always ready to do anything if the money was right.

Abdul's father was a powerful Iranian and his mother was a treasured beauty from a powerful family of Saudi-Arabia. This gave Abdul a foot hold in both of these powerful and turbulent countries. The only thing that could bring him down at this point in his life was the obsessive act of kidnaping the three flowers. The girls and their tribe had been precious to many people of Afghanistan. There was still, after four months, constant cries for retaliation against the people who had done such a monstrous thing. So far no one had pointed their finger at Abdul. He was still obsessed with the idea of producing children from the three young girls that he thought of as women. Abdul had the girl's family lines traced. They were decedents of the most powerful royal families of the Middle Eastern Arabia Countries.

Abdul wanted to be World Dictator, Ruler or King whatever it was the people of the world would accept as the title. But he realized he did not have enough years of life ahead of him to gain the popular appeal of the people, and he also came with too much baggage. If he could not be World King, he would produce the one who would be. He wanted one of his sons, produced from one of the three Flowers, to be Dictator of the World. Abdul thought he could make it happen. He just had to keep it a secret that the girls were alive. He had not had time to travel to his farm. He had decided it might be better to stay away and not draw attention to his hidden mountain retreat. Abdul thought of the young girls as slowly ripening fruit. He would be with them soon in America. They were now waiting in England. The forged travel documents for Jaya, the children and the three flowers that were listed as his wives, would be ready in the next few days. His jet was standing at ready to take them to New York City.

Abdul would not come to the city for at least three to four months. He needed to wait until all the uproar was over about the massacre of the Flowers village. He could not believe how much was still being said about it. Everywhere he went in the Middle East, Abdul either heard comments or read about it in the newspapers. The stories about the people of that tribe and all the wonderful things they had been involved in to help advance the people of Afghanistan and the surrounding countries was being told over and over. It was keeping the massacre in the forefront of everyone's mind. Abdul just had to wait it out.

CHAPTER 12

Allie had been working on the apartments everyday with Gwyn and Peggy helping. The two apartments were amazing homes. They were set up the same with just a slight change to the entrances or placement of rooms. Jaya's apartment was beautiful. When you opened the front door, you entered a half moon shaped entrance hall with pink Italian marble floors and a large crystal chandler hanging in a reset ceiling. Allie had found a large round antique pink marble top table with a heavily carved base. There was a pair of double doors in the back of the entrance hall that opened to a spacious corridor that led into a large living room and formal dining room that had floor to ceiling windows. Allie purchased two amazing paintings of snowcapped mountains with sheep grazing and added soft lighting to shine on them. They were placed on either side of the hallway to the living room for Jaya to enjoy, as a remembrance of the mountains she had traveled from to come to New York. There were heavy wooden doors that lead down halls on either side of the main corridor.

The one on the right lead to the children's three rooms and then to Jaya's master suit. The paint colors thru out the rooms were soft pink tones with chestnut brown wood trim molding. There was lots of recessed lighting down the halls and in every room. Everything was set for an elegant lay out.

The master suit was an amazing retreat from the stresses of life. This apartment was on the end of the building and the master bedroom was at the back corner. It had floor to ceiling windows with a large wide balcony that curved around the outside of the building so you could enjoy the sun or shade at any time of day. Allie ordered outside sofa's, lounge chairs, rockers and a table set for brunch on a warm morning. She also ordered shade trees in large deep cobalt blue pottery planters to space around the area. All of the balcony items would be here early in the morning.

A local New York designer had furnished the master bedroom when the apartment was being shown to interested buyers. The furniture was simply perfect for the big dramatic bedroom with a magnificent view of Central Park. Allie arranged to purchase all of it. She just had to add a few more beautiful things to make it exactly right. The drapes on the large windows were a soft peach color in raw silk and they were attached to a remote-control curtain rod hidden by beautiful ornately curved wooden valances. With the push of a button Jaya could close them in the evening or close them just a little to shade the room for an afternoon nap. The antique heavily carved king size poster bed had two large Chinese's painted chests at either side for large lamps and deep drawers. There was a large sofa in the same fabric as the drapes with two beautiful Asian inspired chairs and tables. All the lamps in the room were Italian majolica porcelain with cherub and flowers in bright colors. Allie ordered towels, sheets, and pillows from the best limen supplier in N.Y.C. for all three bedrooms and bathrooms. The linens had been delivered that morning and were piled all over Jaya's sofa. Allie would wash all the linens in her homemade soap that she had shipped to the apartment. It was hypo-allergenic and smelled like spring. It would add a fresh clean smell to the apartment. The bedrooms and all the living spaces were almost complete. The apartments would be complete when the family arrived. That was one of the many wonderful things about being in the most amazing city in the world. You could find anything you needed or wanted just a few blocks down the street.

Allie felt a connection to Jaya and did not know why. Life was funny sometimes with what it throws at you. She was actually excited to meet Jaya.

All three wives were staying remarkably busy making the arrangements for the family.

Women like women do, were having a fun time planning for the family's arrival as if it were a big gala happening. Not having to worry about now much any purchase cost made it easy to find the best of the best. There was also a since of revenge at spending money that might have been used for terrible wars and senseless killing verses antique oil paintings and children's toys.

Having a bottomless bank account to pull from was loads of fun. So, the three women shopped till they dropped for over two weeks. The apartments look like a magazine cover.

The three husbands on the other hand, had been setting at the hotel waiting to hear from the wives about any word of Abdul's showing up.

The three men had gathered for dinner. It had been two and a half weeks since they had first seen and talked to their wives on the tv screen set up at Allie's house. They could not think of one reason not to make a surprise trip to the State's to see their wives.' They had planned to stay out of the states till they knew something of Abdul's plans. But after seeing the women they loved, the men agreed it had been too long a separation.

They gathered their few belongings and went straight to the airport to start the journey back from no man's land to the women and country they loved. It would take them a few days, but these wanderers were going home.

Gwyn, Peggy, and Allie walked into the hotel lobby chatting and laughing after a fun day of spending more of Abdul's money. Moser had dropped by the apartments to inspect the progress and brought each of them their paycheck with a large bonus. He was amazed at the beauty and origination of the massive project they had undertaken and accomplished in each two weeks. The apartments were luxurious and comfortable at the same time. He told them that the clients would be very satisfied. So, they could call that part of the project finished until the family arrived. And that was to happen on Monday evening late. Moser wanted Gwyn, Allie, and Peggy to come to meet the family on Tuesday, he would let them know the time on Monday.

The wives were planning to take in a Broadway play, if they could get seats this late in the day.

They were looking around for the desk clerk to check for them.

Three hard lean muscled men all stood up at once from the wife's favorite people watching sofa in the side lobby. All the sudden there was a mad race to see who could get to the other faster. All eyes in the lobby watched with smiles as the three couples embraced. Their lives started again at that sweet touch of a second change at love.

There was nothing to say as a group. It was now between wife and husband. It would be room services, lots of talk and loving to night for these happy people.

CHAPTER 13

Kevin had arrived in Boston with no difficulties. The private jet that had flown him to America was registered to a banking firm out of New Zealand. The pilot and crew were of Middle Eastern decent. They greeted him in French but spoke Arabic to one another. When they landed in Boston the crew spoke in perfect English to the refueling crew and passport agent who came to the plane to check in another important rich foreigner. Kevin Stones' paperwork was in order, and his new car registered in his name, had been driven out to the plane for his ease. He walked off the plane and climbed into a new black BMW sports coup. The flight attendant placed his bags in the trunk of the car for him and waved goodbye.

Kevin followed the signs out of the small private airport and entered the fast traffic of life in the U.S. He felt giddy with the overwhelming feeling of freedom. He suddenly realized that he actually was a little lightheaded and dizzy. Kevin pulled over at a small Mom and Pop restaurant and parked on the side of the building to just sit and think for a few minutes. He was overjoyed at being really alone for the first time in over seven long years. He breathed in deeply that great new car and leather smell. The interior was soft chocolate brown and the dash looked like the cock pit of the jet he had just stepped off. The new car smell must be what heaven smelled like, he thought. It was as close to heaven as Kevin would ever be.

He got out of the car and went into the restaurant to order a big juicy hamburger with lots of fries and a large cold beer. He was going to do this job for the money and then take a long vacation. He wanted to go down to the Florida Keys. He might even stop at Disney World and Universal Studios. The flight attendant on the jet had handed him a magazine on tourist destinations in the United States and Kevin had read it from the front to the back page. He really wanted to go somewhere warm for a while and set on a sunny beach. He was not going to push his luck and leave the United States. He planned to stay here for a long time.

Kevin felt better after eating. He decided to find a hotel and rest for a few days. He had not realized how tired he truly was. The friendly waitress told him about a nice, clean bed and breakfast just down a few blocks down the street. She cut him a large slice of pecan pie to go, and Kevin left her the biggest tip she had ever gotten.

He followed the directions he was given and found the comfortable looking bed and breakfast in an old residential neighborhood that looked like a street from his hometown in Ireland. They put the exhausted traveler in a large quite bedroom upstairs in the back of the house. He told the kind elderly lady at the desk not to disturb him. He wanted to sleep and relax for a while. She told him dinner would be served at seven, but if he would rather, they would bring a tray to his door. He told her to just leave it at by the door and he would get it when he was ready. Kevin slept for two days, only waking for the wonderful homemade food left at his door. On the third morning he took a long hot shower and dressed in his fresh cleaned cloths that the maid had taken, washed, and ironed. Kevin decided to go shopping for new cloths. He came downstairs to the smell and visual of all types of wonderful foods lining the beautiful antique sideboard. He was greeted with happy enthusiasm from the staff of Irish transplants. They had all been waiting impatiently to hear this stranger tell his life story as all

Irishman do. They served him hot coffee and fresh eggs from the kitchen and filled his plate with cakes and fresh fried trout.

The elderly husband and wife that owned the B&B were at the desk when he came down to the dining room. They were glad to see their guest looking refreshed and out of his room that needed cleaning. Kevin had paid them in cash the first evening and now paid them for two more nights. The couple called him a cab to take him shopping, explaining that he might have a challenging time finding the shops in the heavy traffic around Boston and then finding his way back to the Olive Branch Bed and Breakfast. Kevin knew the little gray-haired lady was right and decided to follow her motherly advice. The wonderful elderly couple greeted the cabby and introduced him to Kevin, as if Kevin was a long-lost cousin. The cabby, whose name is Martin, was handed a mug of fresh hot coffee and a chocolate cupcake to enjoy as they exchanged info on the weather, the slow economy, and the ware about of family members. All of which took about three minutes as Kevin stood and waited with a smile on his face. The driver was told where to take Kevin, as if Kevin, was the old couples son. They never would have guessed the evil that lurked just under the surface of their borders skin.

Kevin found everything he needed in record time. With the excellent help of the elderly cabby who explained that he was a cousin of the B&B couple. The cabby chatted on as he pointed out the historical sits, they passed by in the city of Boston. Kevin's mind was in a mode that he did not understand. He felt a since of contentment. He suddenly realized it was freedom. He could go anywhere in America. He already had a great deal of cash. He would need to be careful with how fast he spent it. He would do the job in New York and be set for the rest of his life with the money that was to have paid him. He decides to have them send another two hundred thousand just before he killed the man he was going after. He would have the kill all set up. Kevin did not want the group that had gotten him this far, to back out on the money end after he had done the kill. He thought they should be afraid to do that. Because he would find them and kill them if they shorted him. Life and deals were all a gamble. You never knew where any path would take you. Right now, Kevin was ready for a cold beer and some pizza. Martin said he knew just the place. And Martin did.

It was the best pizza and beer Kevin had in his life.

CHAPTER 14

Allies cell phone started ringing early at six in the morning. She and Edward were wrapped up in each other's arms with Edwards long legs thrown over Allie as if he was afraid, she might disappear. He had many dreams like that over the last year. He would never be caught up in another game like this again. He wanted to go home and see the kids and his parents. But the mission was not finished yet.

Allies purse was on the nightstand beside the bed. She had to do the usual search thru the bottomless bag to find the slim pink phone.

It was Moser, Abdul's lawyer. Moser quickly apologized for the early morning call. He and his family were leaving for Florida and had to be at the airport shortly. He wanted to let Allie know that the third apartment deal had gone thru and if the girls wanted to start decorating it, they could begin today. The keys would be with the doorman at the entrance to the building. Jaya a woman from the mountains of Afghanistan was now the owner of three amazing apartments which covered the whole third floor of a beautiful building in Manhattan. This apartment would be Abdul's residents when he was in town and the guards would have their living quarters there also. Moser wanted the apartment set up and ready for the guards and Abdul by Thursday of the following week. Could Allie, do it?

Allie waited a moment to think it thru. She needed to get as much information from Moser as possible. He was not being as secretive as usual because he was distracted with trying to get out the door for his family vacation. She asked when the family was going to arrive in New York City. Moser said the women and children were leaving England Monday evening around eight at night. They would arrive at the apartments about nine Tuesday morning.

Allie asked, "well there be other people besides the family?"

Moser said, "yes there will be two guards and two servants. I would like the three of you to welcome them and explain the working of their new homes. You will get triple pay for the time spent on Abdul's apartment."

Allie said, "I want triple pay for Gwyn and Peggy as will, I will need lots of help to get this done."

Moser quickly agreed to the money, after all, it wasn't his money. He said, "no problem, pay yourselves out of the expense account. I will have my secretary write up the increase in salary to the three of you."

Allie agreed to start immediately on the third apartment. Allie said, "not a problem, we will get the job done."

Moser left for Florida a content man.

Allie would start with the master suite and rooms for the staff. This apartment was totally empty of furnishings and the kitchen had to be stripped and remodeled. Allie's mind was going in overtime as she put her phone down. Then Edward wrapped his strong arms around Allie and pulled her back against his warm body. They had made hard passionate; I need you love several times during the night. This time it would be the, I will never let you out of my site love. Allie happily realized there were more important things in her life again then remodeling a kitchen.

Life was amazing again. Thank you, God.

The three happy couples had agreed to meet for the buffet brunch at eleven in the hotel restaurant. Everyone was starving after their happy reunions. The men had not seen so much wonderful breakfast food in a year. The husbands made several return trips to the long tables full of fruits, breads, and anything else you could think of. Breakfast brunch for these warriors was on Abdul.

Allie had planned to take a quick weekend trip to, Willow Farm. She was home sick for her children and now Edward could not wait to take a quick trip with Allie to see the kids and his parents. Edward had contacted his parents shortly after talking to Allie and ended their joyful talk with Edward explaining that they had to keep his coming, hush hush, to keep the mission safe. The kids were troopers and would follow the no tell orders as well as Edward's parents.

Allie had made her plans last week to leave N.Y.C. at six Saturday night. Edward was able to get a seat on the same flight. They would come back early Tuesday morning in time to be at the apartment with Gwyn and Peggy to welcome Jaya and the family at the apartments.

Allie had called the construction crew to meet her at the third apartment at one o'clock today.

This apartment had been lived in for about a year and a half. Everything would have to be replaced in the kitchen because of religious restrictions of preparing food. She would leave them with detailed instruction of ripping out the kitchen and redoing it. Allie needed Gwyn and Peggy to check out all the other rooms with her and decide what walls had to be painted and what had to be done to floors and bathrooms. Gwyn and Peggy would continue with the remodeling while Allie was gone. They could start ordering furniture and all the accessories that would go into finishing the third apartment. The construction noise would not interfere with Jaya and her family. Most of the noisy work of tearing out the kitchen would be completed by Sunday. It was walls away from Jaya's rooms and the other wives would just have to put up with a little hammering and bumping next door for a few days. It was lots better than the sound of gun fire.

Allie, Gwyn, and Peggy would never understand now much Jaya would appreciate the amazing safe sanctuary of beauty and peace that had been so thoughtfully prepared for her. They were to become her most treasured friends.

The crew would work around the clock doing the construction of a new very modern kitchen. All the appliances were being replaced with the best restaurant grade equipment. All the walls in every room were being painted in bronze browns and sandy tans. The hardwood floors that were in all the living areas were being cleaned and polished. The drapes would be taken down and donated to salvation army along with the used kitchen appliances. The huge windows would be cleaned and polished along with every inch of the apartment.

An oriental rug dealer, by the name of Julia, met the wives at the third apartment at two o'clock to measure the rooms for more of the amazing rugs she had supplied to the other apartments. Everything was already under way. When money was not an object and the rule of the game was the more expensive the better, everything could be accomplished in record time.

At four in the afternoon Allie and Edward left for the airport hand in hand to go for their quick reunion at home. Gwyn and Peggy decided shortly after that, it was time to go find their men and leave the construction to the crew to their work.

The husbands had checked out the finished apartments and the security systems that would be completed by Monday afternoon. The husbands needed to know the lay outs of the rooms. They had also walked over the job in process of the third home. The lay outs of the three apartments were the same. It was the, almost that could throw a monkey wrench into the situation if gun play came into the action of taking down Abdul. This murders time was running out.

CHAPTER 15

Kevin had a restless night's sleep. A gusty freezing wind from Boston Harbor had hammered the B & B and rattled the windows during the night. He lay half-awake listening to the sounds of the household starting the day. The occasional sound of a thumping hum from a passing car or truck on the street out front, penetrated the walls of the big house and traveled thru to Kevin's room. He heard the creaking of the century old wooden floors as the heat was turned up and the chill of the night worked its way out of the historic structure. Somewhere downstairs a door slammed shut. It was the kitchen help coming in to begin cooking for the big meals of the day.

It was early Saturday morning. Four couples had checked in last night. Kevin wanted to be gone before any of them came down for breakfast and a chat. He had packed his bags before turning in last night. He knew he needed to leave because he was starting to feel up tight and closed in. These were some of the kindest people Kevin had ever been around. He did not want to hurt any of them like he had old Tim at the prison. The best thing for him to do was to go quietly before anyone was up. He was paid up thru Monday and would let the extra money be their tip. He threw on his cloths and packed his razor, toothbrush and a few other things that were scattered about the room. He looked at himself in the bathroom mirror and was amazed at how different he looked after the rest and home cooked food. He was also feeling the effects of freedom. It was like taking a deep lung filling breath of ocean air. It renewed his spirt and cleared his mind. He would never risk losing his freedom again. He was going to check this job out and not do it if he could not get safely away. He did want the money. Cash was always a big part of staying free.

Kevin went quietly down the stairs and out the front door. It was about six in the morning, and it looked like a beautiful day for the drive to New York City. He would be there by noon. He climbed into his great car and left with a roar of the powerful motor. His rooms in a luxury hotel had been arranged for him. He was on the fourth floor and faced the apartment complex where the hit had a home with family members. Photos and more information of Abdul and the family were to be delivered to him at the hotel by private messenger tonight.

Kevin was looking forward to seeing the city he had only seen on tv or read about in books and magazines. It had not taken as long to get to the city as he had anticipated, but now he was stuck in the heavy traffic of weekend visitors. His cars G.P.S. delivered him to the hotels entrance after two hours of sitting in traffic. The doorman helped Kevin with his bags and directed him to the check in desk. The doorman took the car keys from Kevin and called for car pick up. The car would be parked in the hotel garage. Kevin would find his car and check out the car exits tomorrow. He was taken to his room where his bags were already waiting for him. The bag boy opens the French doors that lead out to the balcony to show Kevin the view of the busy city. Kevin pulled out a generous tip and said, "thanks." The balcony looked down on the entrance of the apartment building across the street. Kevin's fourth floor room was directly across from the fourth floor of apartments on the other side of the street. He watched as what looked like a crew of twelve or more delivery and construction people entered the front door of the apartment building. The doorman grew weary of holding the door open for the men. He positioned it to stay open and walked back into the lobby. Kevin knew the apartments were being remodeled for Abdul's family and imagined it could possibly be where the boxes of items were going. How lucky was that for him! He was dressed in jeans, tee shirt and dark baseball cap like the crew of workers carrying the furniture and boxes. He would just pick up a box and walk in behind the others.

Kevin hurried out of the hotel, stepped quickly into the endless stream of people, and weaved his way thru them to the end of the block. He crossed the street at the light, which made a quick walk to the open doors of the delivery truck. Kevin just reached in, picked up two lamps and walked into the amazing apartment building lobby. The Marble floors with huge crystal chandeliers twinkling above was amazing enough, but the eye catcher was in the center of the entrance. A twelve-foot-tall bronze mermaid stood with her arms reaching toward the sky in a twisting leap into the air. She was positioned in the middle of a beautiful huge marble water fountain. The sound of the softly splashing water shut out the traffic sounds outside. The doorman pointed to the hallway leading to the service elevator and said, "forth floor to the left." Kevin obeyed the directions with a smile. By the time the doors to the elevator opened on the fourth floor, Kevin had stepped back into his role as predator. He stood for a moment to listen to the sounds coming from the hallway. Female voices and laughter came from the right. As he stepped out into the hall two women were standing in front of the apartment owners' elevator.

He had to take a quick look at the two happy beauties. One glanced his way and saw the lamps. She said, "Peggy looks at the beautiful lamps. Those are going on the tables on either side of the bed in the master bedroom." Gwyn walked over to Kevin to take a closer look at the colors in the porcelain base. The two women smiled at Kevin and told him where to put the lamps until the rest of the furniture arrived. Gwyn and Peggy stepped back to the elevator just as the doors opened and, in a moment, they were gone. Only the light sense of their perfume was left floating in the air.

Kevin walked slowly down the hall there the sounds of voices and hammering were coming from. He stepped thru the open doorway into the apartment. He walked with a self-confident swagger, thru the entrance hall and took a left turn into a side hallway away from the construction sounds.

He had luckily ended up in the area of the bedrooms. Kevin pushed doors slowly open as he advanced down the wide carpeted hallway. The smell of fresh paint and freshly cleaned rooms, along with the new furniture that was sitting around half unpacked, was as good as the new car smell. Kevin wandered thru the amazing bedrooms and bathrooms making a mental check as to the size and any unusual hiding places that he could use in his job of killing this man, Abdul. He was still carrying the lamps. As he entered the master bedroom Kevin almost bumped into a latter with a man standing next to the top rung. The man was concentrating on his job of installing a series of small cameras that made a circle in the center of the ceiling, so all angles of the room could be viewed. Abdul enjoyed viewing his sexual encounters with people besides his wives. He was known as the Lion, by the Call Girl Agency's he frequented in New York City. They would only send their most seasoned, hard-core women or men to spend time with him. The Agency was paid tremendous amounts of money from Abdul's endless supply from his backers, for his viscous sexual habits. This room would be Abdul's safe haven and sex arena.

Kevin placed the lamps on the floor in a corner and then continued his casing out of the huge set up of rooms. He took photos with his phone camera of windows, doors, and the large wraparound outside pool and patio. The workers all around him were absorbed in their jobs.

They never questioned him as to who he was or what he was doing in the apartments. Kevin wandered methodically throughout every room and closet. He found Allie's notebook with her diagrams of the furniture set-ups for each room on the huge dining room table. He flipped back to an empty page and started drawing out his own plans for easiest entrance and exit of the apartment.

Soft female voices interrupted Kevin's thoughts. laugher and the higher twinkling sounds of girl talk mixing with the deep voices of the male workers was coming from somewhere toward the front of the apartment. He heard the word, notebook and realized he was most likely holding the one they were searching for. He quickly tore the page out of the notebook he had been writing on, closed it, and placed it back on the table where he had found it. Kevin then started making his way back up the apartment hallway, weaving thru the congestion of ladders and box's and away from the voices. These women were most likely the ones he had already bumped into earlier at the elevator. He did not want anyone becoming familiar with his looks. He did not want to add more kills to this job. It always made a quick escape impossible.

Kevin made it to the open front door, walked to the next apartment and gently turned the large brass handle. To his surprise it opened. This apartment was complete and waiting for its lucky people to arrive and enjoy the heated white marble floors and amazing furnishing. This was obviously the women's housing. It had quite the female look and feel of everything beautiful.

There were colors and fabrics that even Kevin had to stop and admire. He wandered thru out the beautiful rooms and took note of the number and sizes of each one. He was not planning to come back into these spaces, but it was always good to have the lay outs, surrounding a job, checked out. He was now entering the master bedroom. It was obviously the number one wife's retreat. It was amazingly beautiful with all the soft colors, flowing silk fabrics and plush furniture. The bed was a site to behold. The four-poster king bed had flowers and vines carved into the dark mahogany wood with a padded red silk headboard to softly lean her head against as she read a good book. A deep pile of pillows lined the headboard and a heavily embroidered bed spread of deep copper and gold was already turned down, waiting for its mistress to arrive. It was an amazing apartment of access, no cost to high. The money poured into Abdul's pockets with abundance with nobody daring to ask questions as to how it was spent.

Kevin started to feel the rumble of hunger in his body. After years of prison his body was time set with the systems meal routine. It always brought out the animal survival instinct in Kevin, as well as all the other prisoners. Fights would break out quicker over one prisoner looking at someone else's plate and thinking the other man had received a little more mashed potatoes on his plate, then he had been served. The screaming would start then the punches would begin and everyone would be herded from the dining area, and no one would get to eat. If any prisoner got the chance, the food fighters would be dead by morning. No man wanted to miss a meal.

Kevin took a few deep breaths to ease his anxiety and walked slowly back to the front door of the apartment. The thoughts of prison life had made him feel claustrophobic even in this house of beauty. He had to get outside fast, or he was going to do something crazy. He was in an all over sweat and his hands were shaking. Kevin opened the front door of the apartment just a crack and listened only a moment before stepping out and starting down the hall toward the elevator. The door of the elevator swished open from Kevin's persistent button pushing. A young couple with two children were in the elevator on the way to their fifth-floor apartment. With smiles on their friendly faces, they held the door open and invited the devil in for ride. He wanted to step in and wipe the smiles off their stupid faces with the braking of their necks. Lucky for them, Kevin mumbled that he would take the stairs.

In two minutes, Kevin was down the stairs and into the nose and traffic of the big city. He walked fast down the people filled sidewalk with everyone stepping quickly out of the big man's way. The first eatery he came to was everyone's favorite Mc Donald's. At four in the afternoon there was only a short line of people placing orders. Kevin ordered a big mac special and super- sized it, the house salad, the two-apple pie special and a large cup of coffee with two creams and two sugars. He took his order and sat at a table with his back to a wall and facing the front door. He wanted no one behind him and the exit straight in front of him. He hoped he had not lost his vicious, murderous touch.

CHAPTER 16

Jaya 's intense excitement was overwhelming. Her heart was beating so fast it felt as if it was going to going to pop out of her chest. She and her family had been traveling in Abdul's amazingly luxurious jet for almost eight hours. The beautiful and truly kind hostess, whose name was Ruby, had answered every question the children had asked, which was many, for the first few hours of flight time. She finally just sat with the children, specking to them in their own language and telling them of the things she had learned about the amazing country of America.

She had traveled to many of the cities in America with their father, Master Abdul. It was a wonderful county, with New York City being the most incredible city in the world. She sat with the children till they fell asleep with smiles on their faces. Happy from listening to her fun tells of the country they were to call home.

Then she turned her attention on Jaya and the three flowers. She told them to stay in America at all costs. The U.S.A. was the only safe haven in the world. It was a huge country that a person could get lost in.

Jaya asked Ruby where she was from. She told them the too familiar tale of being taken in one of Abdul's murderous raids on her village. She was now a slave to Abdul. He had butchered her family and most of the village families. Ruby told them know she had been married just over a year to a fine man and they had a two-month-old baby boy.

Abdul's thuds had stormed into their small village after midnight, when everyone was home and in bed. He took all the men and boys of her village, which included her young husband, on this vicious raid out into the street. He lined them up and shot them in front of their families.

Abdul ordered the heads cut off some of the men and boys and had them placed on tall stakes at the entrance of the village. The women and children left alive were standing, setting, or laying on the ground in a state of shock. They were screaming, crying, or just quietly staring in shock at what remained of their loved ones.

Abdul ordered the screamers shot and removed from the group. The remaining women were lined up in front of their murdered families. Abdul, of course was the first to choose his newest group of slaves. He chose the most attractive and healthiest women for himself. As Abdul walked down the line of crying women and children, he pointed without a word to the ones he would take, then his men would drag them out to the waiting trucks. When he came to Ruby, he stopped and looked at her and then at the sleeping child in her arms. He asked her if it was a boy or girl and her silence told him it was a boy. Abdul held out his hands to take the beautiful child from Ruby. She had no choice. She handed her heart over with her child. His men watched as Abdul took the warm little bundle and placed it next to the wall of one of the houses. There was not a sound as the thugs and remaining villagers watched him.

Abdul strutted, consumed with the evil of the moment, back to Ruby putting his face against her terrified one and with a loud demonic laugh said loudly for all to hear, "the dogs will have a tasty treat today." He then slapped Ruby so hard across the face, it mercifully knocked her out. She was then dragged to Abdul's truck with his other choices.

Ruby ended her life story with a shrug as a few tears escaped her large almond shaped eyes and ran down her beautiful young face.

The three flowers went to the young women and took her hands in theirs to comfort her and called her sister. Jaya did not move or speak. She was too much in mourning for the lives lost because of evil men like Abdul. She closed her eyes as a tear slide down her cheek.

There was a series of soft beeping sounds in the planes cabin. It was the pilots putting Ruby on notice to get her passengers ready for landing in about forty-five minutes. Ruby stood up with a sad smile on her lovely face. It was the best she could manage after reliving her horrible nightmare with them. It had been almost a year sense Abdul and these murderous monsters had come and killed her family. Ruby now had trouble remembering her past life, with a loving husband and their beautiful baby boy. It seemed more like a pleasant dream. Being with women from like circumstance, all their family and friends murdered by the same devil going by the name, Abdul.

Ruby started gathering the uneaten food and drinks. She tightened the seat belts around the sleeping children and watched as Jaya and the girls buckled up. Jaya did not know the answer to this human atrocity, but she would correct it the best she way could. Ruby was now part of her family. Ruby would come with them in New York City.

The plane started its smooth decent to American soil and American laws and rules. Jaya felt a power of strength flow thru her. It was a feeling she had never felt before. It was her job to protect her little family and she would.

The jet landed with a gentle bump of the wheels to the smooth runway as the powerful engines roared into reverse to slow the fast-moving plane to a rolling stop at the entrance of the terminal gates. The bright yellow glow of the morning sun started its, welcome to America shine, as the plane door was pushed open.

Ruby helped the family gather their bags and held the children's hands as they descended the tall stairs to the ground. A large black limousine was pulling up to the group as they stood on the runway getting there first glimpse of America.

The pilots and other stewardess were also getting off for a sleep- over from the long flight. Ruby held out her hand to wish the family good-by as the limousine driver finished loading the bags into the trunk of the big car.

The other stewardess brought Ruby's small travel bag from the plane and handed it to her, since Ruby had been busy helping the children. The crew stayed together at a nearby hotel and were now loaded in a taxi waiting for Ruby.

Jaya told Ruby to get into the limousine with the children, Ruby hesitated for just a moment before climbing in after the children.

One of the pilots immediately hopped out of the taxi and run over to the car. Jaya told him that they were taking Ruby with them to help with the children. Jaya told the pilot to give Ruby's passport to her immediately.

The pilot stood for a moment, trying to decide if there would be any negative repercussions toward him from Abdul if he allowed Ruby to go with Jaya. He looked into the car at all the happy faces. Ruby was sitting between the two young children and each child held a hand. He placed his briefcase on the back of the car and pulled Ruby's passport from it. He then handed Ruby's passport to freedom, into the kind hands of Jaya.

The pilot went back to the taxi got in with the others. The crew drove away without looking back.

The driver took Jaya's hand and helped her into the big back seat of the beautiful car, closing the door with a thud. She felt as if she had taken a small stand against the rule of Abdul and all the evil men that she and her new family had suffered under. They would start a new life together as a family, in America.

CHAPTER 17

Jaya's mind was in a tired twirl of a mixture of childlike excitement one minute and then fear and anxiety the next. She had never been told anything about where they were going or the type of life they would have. It was not that she placed any trust in Abdul, it was that she had no other life experience to base how good or bad this would turn out.

They had crossed a long bridge that had cars and trucks whizzing by at a steady blur. There driver was moving them quickly to whatever life Abdul had chosen for them.

Jaya wished she were home on the farm. It was always easier to stay with the same existence no matter now bad, then to jump off that cliff to something new. The whole family was diffidently being pushed toward a huge change of lifestyle.

They were now in the busy streets of New York City. The family listened to Ruby's explanation of where they were and what they were seeing. Their driver told them that they were almost to their home and that people would be ready to help them with everything they would need to know. The limousine pulled up in front of the amazing apartment complex that would be their new home. Jemal, one of the two house servants was standing in front of the entrance to the building waiting for the family's arrival. He was at the curb before the car could come to a stop. He opened the door and held out his hand to help the ladies out of the car. He immediately questioned Jaya about the additional women in their party. She told him it was none of his business to question her in bringing another relative to help with the children. Jaya stood as tall as her five-foot three frame could stand and gave him her toughest mother tiger stare. Jemal glared back but lost the battle. Jaya would not be bullied any more.

She turned her back on Jemal, gathered her family and instructed Jamal to lead the way to their new home.

It was about eight thirty on a beautiful sunny morning in The Big Apple. People were busy going to work, shopping or just site seeing. The streets were full of the usual beeping traffic of cars, trucks of every size and bicycles were weaving thru the congestion. The family stood on the sidewalk for a moment, savoring the hustle and bustle of life in this amazing city. Jemal was standing at the entrance door of the apartment building. He gave a slight bow to Jaya as she entered last. He hurried to show them the way to the elevator. But the family was standing open mouthed, staring at the huge fountain of shimmering water playing over the amazing mermaid statue. Jaya finally called to the women and children to come and follow Jemal.

Jaya and her children had only been in an elevator twice and that was in London at a department store. Jaya had found the experience slightly unnerving. The children had delighted in the quick ride. The children had run to tell the flowers about the experience and the girls had shared that they had ridden in elevators many times on trips with their families. This elevator was a large space with mahogany paneling and a small bench with a golden-brown velvet cushion on top. There was a beautifully done oil painting on the back wall of a large lake surrounded by snowcapped mountains. The elevator door opened with a whisper into a wide spacious hallway. There was thick carpeting with amazing hand loomed rugs of deep reds, dark blues, and bright coral pinks. The busy designs in the rugs explained different meanings in the tribal lives in Afghanistan. The walls were painted a forest green. Plush satin covered sofas and chairs lined the walls. Heavily carved side tables of polished mahogany were topped with expensive antique treasures. Large porcelain lamps and recessed lighting made the hallway just a taste of what was to come in the family's new homes.

Jaya was quivering with anticipation as well as exhaustion from all she had been through.

Jamal explained to the family as they gazed at the amazing beauty around them, that the family owned the hallway and the four apartments. This floor of apartments had been purchased by Abdul for his use when he was in the U.S.

Jamal had not noted the American ladies standing at the entrance of Jaya's new home. He had been specking in their tribal tongue. Allie asked him to repeat what he had said in English. He hesitated just long enough that Lilly stepped forward and told the wives that Jamal had told them they would be living in apartments owned by Abdul.

Allie told Lilly to explain to Jaya that everything she was about to see, including the hallway was owned by her alone. Plus, lots of money in a bank account, which was Jaya's to use anyway she choose.

Lilly stepped close to Jaya, took her hand, and repeated what the American women had said.

Jaya sank down to the floor in a half faint of unbelief.

Allie, Gwyn, and Peggy rushed to Jaya and helped her to her feet.

Allie took charge of Jaya and her children with Ruby following into the apartment that was designed for them.

Gwyn and Peggy took the three young women one door down the hall to their new home.

Allie did a walk around tour with Jaya as her two children clung to her hands. Allie could see that the young women called Ruby, was paying closer attention to her short instructions then Jaya. The massive lay-out of the fabulous apartment with its many luxurious rooms was overwhelming to the road weary Jaya. It had been a strange and exhausting journey for this mother, farmer, and family leader.

The wives told the family to eat the wonderful foods prepared for them and rest. Allie, Peggy, and Gwyn told them that they would return in the afternoon at four to check on everyone.

Jaya looked at Allie and said in broken English that she wanted to take a hot bath in the huge, amazing tub. Allie showed Jaya where everything was and how it worked.

While Jaya was enjoying her bath, Allie went to the large closet and took one of the numerous soft cotton night gowns and robe sets and laid it on the bed.

Allie went in search of the children and the young women. She found Ruby with the children in their toy filled bedrooms.

Ruby explained to Allie that Jaya had hired her to help with the children. That she had been a stewardess on Abdul's jet. Allie could tell there was more to the story than this brief explanation by the sadness that showed in Ruby's beautiful, young face.

Allie said, "If Jaya is happy, I'm happy."

"Let's look at the rooms we designed for a servant's private quarters." Allie showed Ruby the spacious rooms that were convenient to the children's rooms and opened to the kitchen. Ruby even had a small private balcony off her bedroom, which looked out over the busy streets of New York City. Ruby was speechless at the amazing apartment in an apartment. Tears filled her lovely dark eyes. A big smile was working its way to the surface of her sweet face. Allie noted that Ruby had only a small carry-on suitcase. Allie said" we have lots of money and will start shopping for whatever you need in cloths and extras tomorrow."

Allie could see that Ruby would be of immense help to Jaya and the children as well as to the three of them in getting things set up for the family in their new home, America. Jaya and her family understood, as well as spoke some English, but needed help expressing their ideas. Ruby was just what the family and Allie needed to bridge that gap.

Gwyn and Peggy had enjoyed the three teenage girls and their excitement in being in the city. The wives were amazed to find out that it was not the girls first trip to stay and shop in N.Y.C., as well as in many other places in the U.S. Gwyn and Peggy had left Daisy, Rose and Lilly getting ready for a hot shower and nap with the promise of dinner and maybe a movie tonight.

The husbands had lots of info on the family members, but had wanted Allie, Gwyn, and Peggy to meet the people involved before developing mental baggage about them. The women were all displaced people from a dysfunctional country. The horrific events that brought them under Abdul's thumb were happenings out of their control. Allie said a silent prayer, thanking God for the opportunity to help these women have a peaceful and safe life.

CHAPTER 18

Abdul wanted to fly to New York by the end of the week. But the Imam's had different plans. They financed his high living ways and expected him to jump when they said jump. The imams' sent word for Abdul to be in Dubai for a series of meeting with the heads of several tribes from Iran, Afghanistan, and Iraq. The gathering was to last at least two weeks maybe longer depending on the co-operation of the Tribal Chiefs involved.

The three flowers were never far from Abdul's mind. He was burning with desire for their sweet young bodies. He would be with no other women till he had bedded the three girls and had them carrying his son's.

The Imam's would have Abdul's head removed from this body, if they ever found out that the girls were still alive and being kept in the U.S. with their money. It would be impossible to keep peace among the tribes if the girls were found alive and told what had happened to the beloved people of their village.

If it was discovered that the Imam's had contracted Abdul to destroy the village and its people nothing would stop the horrific tribal war that would follow. Abdul was walking a tight complicated rope with all his deception. He was letting his passion for the power he had convinced himself he would receive, if he produced children with Lilly, Rose, and Daisy. He would just have to wait a little longer.

CHAPTER 19

Amiee and Mazie had finished their fall semester at Auburn University and were flying to New York to send time with their Mom and Dad. Just being able to say "Dad" could still fill their eyes with tears. They needed more time with him to feel that he was real. Their parents had spent a quick weekend with them in Auburn, so the shock of the amazing news of Tom being alive had soften a little. But as they walked thru the congestion of New York's' busiest airport, the anxiety of such a brutal separation from a loving parent filled them again. Just ahead of the lines of people, they caught a glimpse of their tall, strong, hero Dad. It filled them with overwilling gladness and love. Of course, the tears started flowing, but Tom was there to comfort them. Life was safe and good again.

CHAPTER 20

Jaya and her family were becoming accustomed to life in the Big Apple. There new homes and amazing way of life filled everyone with happy plans for the future. They shopped by day and usually ate out in the evenings. They were settling into a comfortable routine.

The three flowers had become fast friends with Amiee and Mazie. The girls shopped, dinned out or had take-out in one of the amazing apartments. They also did the rounds of the Broadway plays and museums. The girls had a limousine with driver and bodyguard at their beckoning call.

Amiee and Mazie had invited Rose and Daisy to fly back to Alabama with them and meet all their friends and family. Jaya had decided it would be good for Daisy and Rose, but Ruby would need to go as a chaperone. Lilly would move in with Jaya and her children, while the older girls were gone for the week.

There was so much freedom in America. And Jaya wanted the children to feel safe and loved. Gwyn would also be traveling with them. The girls were so much fun to be with. They filled the hallway and apartments with lots of talk, laugher, and the fun of being young.

Gwyn's 'twin daughters had helped Jaya's' people start thinking and acting like a real family. Jaya had heard nothing from Abdul. She was living day by day with the pressure of his coming. She would never allow him to hurt these good people that had become her family. Jaya had always carried a special knife. It was not but eight inches long and just under an inch wide there it joined a bone handle that fit her grip perfectly. The blue steel blade narrowed to just one eight of an inch before it took a slight curve to the right and ended with a razor-sharp tip. One of the men on the farm had made the knife. Jaya had made the leather sheath from the hide of a sheep the men had butchered on the farm. The hide was soft but strong. And the knife slid securely into it at her side. It made her feel strong with determination to protect her family. She would kill Abdul, if she had too.

Abdul had moved another fifteen million dollars into Jaya's bank account in New York. He did not think of it belonging to anyone but him. He owned Jaya; she was no more than a servant to him. Abdul thought it was just a name for the account. He never stopped to think it was not his money anymore.

Abdul was having trouble satisfying the Imam's. It was the first time they had questioned his actions and money expenses. He could see a change coming in this power. Sense the U.S. had all but pulled their support out of Afghanistan, the need for his murderous ways was not anything special. Everyone seemed to be ready to kill at the first off glance or word. Everyone wanted to be the bully.

Abdul was going to New York. He was through jumping to the demands of others. He was smarter, stronger, and wealthier than most and he was ready to be free of this life. When the powers of men changed again, as it all ways did, he would turn back to his murderous ways. And make lots more money, right now he just wanted to spend it.

Danger was coming. Kevin could feel it. Icy fingers of slow-moving air lifted just the tips of the hair on his arms and the back of his neck. The slow swirl of a tingle touch that sent a chilly shiver down his spine. His Irish Grandmother called it the whisper of the death angel. She would tell us to "shoosh" and to listen for the sharp creaking of the gates to hell opening up. "When you hear that sound," she said, "run"!

It is Tuesday morning. Allie and Peggy, with all three husbands are staying in the city for the duration of the mission. Edwards parents have flown up with the children to stay for a week.

Allie is taking them to ice skate and meet Jaya's' family. The group will go for food and hot chocolate after skating. Jaya also wanted to go back to Macys Department Store. Macy's mailed items all over the world. Jaya had already sent lots of clothing, pots and pans and delicious candies and cookies to her family at the farm in Afghanistan.

It is a bright, crisp winters day, with clear blue skies and lots of sunshine. Jaya called for her driver to be ready to take she, Lilly, and the children for a drive around the city. She could not get enough of the Christmas decorations and colorful lighting everywhere. The children and Lilly wanted to try ice skating. Allie had made reservations at The Rockefeller Center, and they were meeting them there. They were going to have fun. Jaya thought, I might try ice skating, too.

The happy group came nosily off the elevator and started thru the lobby. The children were pushing each other to be the one to hold Lilly's hands. She is explaining to the threesome that she only has two hands. The next battle will be who can sit beside her in the car.

Just as they are passing through the lobby doors, the clerk at the front desk calls to Jaya that she has mail. He hurries to her and hands over a note from the farm in Afghanistan. It makes Jaya realize she hasn't been getting any mail. Abdul's man, Jamel must have been collecting and checking with Abdul on anything said from the farm. When she returns from this fun day, Jamel will be out the door.

Kevin was enjoying his super-sized breakfast. The coffee, with lots of cream and sugar, was the best he had very tasted. It went really great with his plate of eggs, pancakes and two orders of bacon.

The clean-up crew were always working to keep everything in order and sanitized. Kevin was absent-mindedly watching the tables being wiped and floor being swiped and moped. A broom left leaning in a corner suddenly, with-out provocation, slide down the wall and hit the floor with a sharp pop-bang. It sounded like a pistol being fired.

One of the cleaning crew made the immediate remark, "someone is coming." Another girl asked, "why did you say that?" The soothsayer said "My Grandmother always told us that it was true. That you were receiving a warning. And you had better to be looking out for a stranger or angry spirt or combination of both.

Kevin knew who the stranger was. Abdul was on his way.

CHAPTER 21

Jaya had spent a painful night after her attempted at ice skating. She felt really stupid for thinking she could step out onto the beautiful, people filled, ice rink and just be a skater. The children had been quick to move from shuffling along to suddenly, after a few falls, to actually be doing a respectable foot over foot movement.

Lilly was amazing. As soon as she stepped out on the ice, she gilded gracefully to the other side of the large rink. Jaya watched as Lilly's beautiful face relaxed, and her young body followed. Ice skating seem to come naturally to the young girl. She was soon maneuvering around the other skaters as if she had been doing this her all her life. xxx

Jaya felt inspired to give it a try.

Allie was in the ring helping the young ones.

So, Jaya went to the skate rental and picked out a pair of red skates in her size. Walked back to their spot on the bleachers and changed from her black boots into the red beauties.

The seats were close to the open gate and Jaya stepped out onto the ice. She made a few shuffling slides before her feet flew out from under her.

Allie saw Jaya go down hard on her left knee, they fall to her side and hit her head with a smack.

Allie and the children, as well as the rink attendants rushed to her side.

Life had taught Jaya not to show pain. In her world if you showed pain or any other emotion you would suffer a beating, because the men in her life saw it as personal weakness.

Allie was at Jaya's side gently holding her hand and telling her she would be okay.

It had taken Jaya a few moments to remember what had happened. The ice was very cold against her body, and she had started to tremble. Jaya had always taken care of herself which made all the attention she was receiving un-nerving. She tried to sit up but could not. Her head did a nauseating spin from the hard hit her head had taken and her ears were ringing.

Jaya was trying to tell everyone that she was fine, but words would not come.

The paramedics arrived and gently lifted her to a rolling bed. It seemed everyone at the rink was anxious about her condition. Her children were clinging to the moving stretcher with their little heads hanging down, so no one could see their tears.

Allie was not only focusing on Jaya, but also on the children and Lilly.

Lilly was instructed to take the twins hands and Allie picked up the little girl. They followed along to the ambulance and found out there they were taking Jaya.

Allie called Peggy and told her what had happened. She asked her to be waiting by the curb to take the children and keep them at the hotel, till they knew about Jaya's condition.

As soon as the children were with Peggy, Allie and Lilly headed to the hospital. Lilly was needed for communication between the doctors and nurses and Jaya. After x-rays the doctors cleared Jaya to go home with her knee and ankle in a soft removeable cast and brace. With instructions to keep the leg propped up and to wake her every hour in case of a concussion from hitting her head. She was given a shot of pain killer, which made her drowsy, but her leg not so painful for the trip home.

Allie and Lilly would stay at the apartment with Jaya. The children were having fun with Peggy and would stay at the hotel for the night.

Edward was uneasy about Allie staying at the apartment. A voice in his head kept whispering, "this could be the night."

Jaya thought she might enjoy the sport of ice skating if she had a few lessons. Her whole body and spirt felt an up lifting of happiness at all the wonderful things she and the children could do. This was what it felt like to think about, fun.

She drifted back in thought to all the hardships and physical work she had been required to do over her lifetime. Thirty-four was as close as she could guess her age to be, give or take a year or two. Jaya thought about the farm and the crops, animals, and the people she had taken care of.

That reminded her of the letter from the farm.

Allie had placed a hand bell on the nightstand by Jaya's' bed, which Jaya did not ever plan to use. Allie was staying in the next room ready to come when ever Jaya needed her. Jaya had true friends in the three women that had come to love and appreciate she and her family in such a short time. There came a soft tap on the door and Allie stepped into the room with a cup of tea and a smile.

Jaya told Allie about the letter in her purse. Jaya notated a snape of attention in Allie, who quickly went in search of the bag. Allie found it with Jaya's discarded coat and hat in the apartment entrance. She quickly returned to Jaya with purse in hand.

Allie busied herself opening the drapes and straightening up the bedroom while Jaya pulled the letter from her small purse, carefully tore the end open and started reading. It was a short read. Allie had stopped doing and was watching Jaya. Jaya looked at Allie and with fear in her eyes said in a whisper "he is coming."

The jet was gilding along so smoothly it had given Abdul a feeling of lightness. The weather had been perfect. In a few more hours he would see and feel the three flowers. He thought he would have the youngest first. She would not be much of a challenge. The other two he would take together and see what he could teach them.

Abdul looked out the window at the vastness of the Atlantic Ocean. It had been a long flight from Dubai. Abdul was deep in thought over his decision to flee from what he could tell was going to be, his head on a platter. Abdul had enough of the remarks and questions about his high handed, murderous actions. He had summoned the flight crew to meet him immediately at one of the many private runways in Dubai. He had to point a gun at the pilots to make them understand that they would fly with one crew member short. Abdul did not care about the regulations of the FFA. Since Jaya had pulled Ruby away from his flight crew, the shifts of stewardess had been messed up. Abdul was going to beat them both.

As soon as the word was out, that he was gone. The man hunt had begun. The Iman's saw the writing on the wall, in the changing of power. They did not want the albatross of Abdul the Lion, hanging around their neck. Because they knew, a rope would be next.

Then decide to send word to the bodyguards in the N.Y., that Abdul was on his way, they wanted him killed at first site and his body disposed of. They wanted no one to ever know that he had defied them and left Dubai.

The group in charge of hiring Kevin had gotten wind of Abduls' coming execution. News like that travels fast. They wired Kevin the full amount of money agreed upon, for the contract killing of Abdul. They did not want a dissatisfied killer with revenge on his mind. They asked him to leave town and the state of N.Y. immediately. That was fine with Kevin. He packed and was in his car in less than an hour. He was heading south to the beaches of Miami.

The pilots radioed ahead for Abdul's car and driver to meet the plane. They then received a message to fly out as soon as their passenger was off the plane and on his way in the car. They were to say nothing about these plans to Abdul. The pilots were to fuel up and fly to Atlanta where they could do their required rest. Then they were to fly straight back to Dubai. The stage was being set for the assassination of an assassin.

CHAPTER 22

Edward and Jack had moved into a room just two doors down from where Kevin had stayed. Kevin had to wait for the two men to exit the elevator, so he could enter and move on to his first chance at being free. He had hopes of being able to fit in with normal people. He was rested. He had eaten lots of good food. And had plenty of money to set himself up in a comfortable lifestyle. Kevin's time away from prison had eased his murderous desirers to inflect pain on others. But wherever he ended up, people would always be in danger of the evil hiding just under his skin.

Edward and Jack were nervous. Having their wives involved in this mission was frightening. The women felt nothing but sympathy and kindness toward Jaya and her family. They thought like Americans. They would never understand the mindset of the evil, dangerous people, who made up the circle surrounding Jaya.

Abdul was wrapped up in his thoughts. He was high on how superior he was in every way to the men he had walked away from. He was in the U.S.A. and had that glorious feeling of having outsmarted everyone. He felt untouchable.

Abdul became lost in his memories of Jaya. She had been so fortunate to have been given to him when she was so young. She had produced three sons that had served him will. The middle boy had been killed in a battle outside of Kabul and the youngest son had lost an eye and suffered neck injuries. He was flown back to the farm. Abdul had no time for an injured son, boy or man. He did not want someone near himself that could be of no use.

The oldest son at twenty-two was most like his father. He was tuff, smart and a survivor. He was already respected by Abduls' army of terrorist. He was the next in line to plan and lead murderous raids on innocent tribes. Abdul thought this son might have a chance of living to see twenty-three.

Abdul decided he would find time to plant his seed deep into Jaya again and see what she could produce.

His main obsession would be the Flowers. They were young and fresh. Abdul would have Jaya and Ruby scrub their skin till it was pink and soft. And shave all the hair from there body, except the amazing black hair on their heads. It would be brushed and perfumed. He enjoyed the feel of it tickling his skin. And it also made an easy grab if she tried to escape his touch. After this visit their heads would be shaved and they would live out their days under a burka as his wives.

The Imams are in charge now. The message had been sent and gladly received by the bodyguards at the apartment. The three Afghans had been living in the apartment beside Jaya's' family as their protectors. They were more than ready to carry out the killing of this monstrous devil. Abdul had tortured and killed many of their family and countryman. He had destroyed villages and their way of life. So many of their family, friends and countrymen had to flee his reign of terror and were now living in in refugee camps in other counties. They would happily reid the world of Abdul the Lion.

The limousine pulled up in front of the apartment building. Abdul did not wait for Jemal to come open the car door. He was excited to start his new life. For a brief moment Abdul did wonder where Jamel might be. He would give him a hard slap across his stupid face as soon as he saw him.

Abdul took a moment to glance at the lobby with the amazing mermaid fountain. He thought, this is nothing, Dubai had so much more to offer. He hoped to go back soon.

Abdul then notices' there is no one at the desk in the lobby and no guards are about. He feels a slight twinge that something is not right. He is trying to decide between walking swiftly back to the limo or what? He walks back to the entrance and the limo is already gone. Abdul hurries to the elevator and takes the short ride to the third floor. He steps out into the beautifully decorated hallway and see's heavy plastic spread over at least ten feet of the carpet and a couple of feet up and over the walls and furniture.

Abdul keeps walking and reaches the middle of the crunchy sounding plastic. Suddenly the thought enters his mind, this looks like a set up for a killing.

The door to the guard's apartment opens and out step his bodyguards, the desk clerk, and the lobby doorman and guard. They were all brought to N.Y. from Afghanistan as Abduls men. He had been pressing his thumb into their heads with threats to their families for years.

They are not his men anymore. They are here to witness his assignation.

The shot to his head and the one to his heart has no more sound, then a cork popping from a champagne bottle.

Abdul's reign of terror is over. The plastic is wrapped around his body, and he is placed on a rolling cart. He is then taken to the service elevator at the end of the hall. His body and the three guards travel down to the garage where his body is placed into a waiting van. The other men taketheir places back in the lobby It will be a short trip to a local funeral home and cremation for Abdul. No evidence will be left of the Lion.

Edward and Jack had seen the limo arrive and Abdul step out and go into the apartment building. They had been drinking a beer and watching from their balcony across the street. The two ran down the hotel stairs two and three at a time. Then rushed out into the busy three lanes of N.Y.C traffic. They noticed that the limo had quickly vanished from its park and wait spot in front of the apartment building. They ran into the lobby and quickly saw that there were no guards are desk clerk.

The elevator showed its third-floor stop.

Edward and Jack tried the door for the stairway walk up, but it is locked. The lobby is empty of any employees. The only sound came from the splashing water of the mermaid fountain.

They know Jaya is the only one at the apartment, accept the bodyguards who will be no protection for her from Abdul. What was going on?

The elevators soft ding as it ascended to the lobby level breaks the silence. Suddenly the doorman is standing at ready, and the desk clerk and bodyguard are at their usual spots.

Jack and Edward ran to the elevator and pushed the button for the third floor. The soft wine of the motor lifting them to Jaya's apartment floor, glides to a stop and the doors softly opens up. The men slowly step out with guns at ready. They look just in time to see the door close on the service elevator at the end of the long hallway. They watch as it descends to the garage.

The bodyguard apartment door has been left slightly open. Jack pushes it wide and he and Edward with guns at ready check out every room and closet. The apartment is empty. There is no sign of the men who had lived here for months. The guards are gone.

Jack and Edward step back into the hallway just as the ding of the elevator sounds. Outcome Jaya's 'three young children and Lilly, with Allie and Peggy following. There happy chatter and laughter stop at the sight of Edward and Jack with guns. The men motion the group to go back to the elevator just as Jaya limps out into the hallway.

The men are caught between the children and their mother. The three children dart around Edward and Jack and run to Jaya. Lilly quickly follows.

The husbands then rush everyone into Jaya's home

With Lilly's help, Jaya says that she had not heard or seen anything. She had been out on the balcony enjoying the sun. Allie had phoned to say she and the children were on their way up. So, Jaya had come to greet them at the front door

Edward carefully checks every room and closet in Jaya's home, while Jack is going over the girl's apartment.

There is no one to be found. Abdul had disappeared.

Jack and Edward decide it's okay to leave the girls, with strict instructions to stay together with Jaya. Allie locks the heavy front door as the men step out into the hallway.

The men look everything over as they move slowly to the service elevator. The doors glide open easily. There is a streak of fresh blood smeared on the elevate wall and drops of blood on the floor. They take the ride to the garage and find more blood drops on the concrete. The spots stop at the point where the vehicle would have been waiting to take the wounded or dead away.

The cameras tell the rest of the story. Edward and Jack watch as Abdul entered the apartment complex, took the elevator to the third floor, walked down the hallway and on to the sheet of plastic. Then the cameras stopped filming for five minutes. The cameras started filming at the same moment Jack and Edward stepped off the elevator. The plastic was already removed, and the hallway appeared as always.

Edward and Jack go back to the service elevator to take another look. It had been wiped clean in the few minutes that it had taken them to watch the film. They quickly check the garage.

Nothing Is left of the assignation. Abdul the Lion is no more.

CHAPTER 23

Rose and Daisy returned from their Alabama visit. They had a wonderful time with Maize and Aimee. The twins had given them the college town tour. They were ready to sign up for fall semester at Auburn University. Gwynn had cooked wonderful southern food for them and enjoyed spending time with all four girls. Rose and Daisy enjoyed the family's big home in Birmingham. They would always be welcome. It was the American way.

Jack and Peggy had flown back to Baltimore. They had made the decision to move south, maybe the mountains of Tennessee. That would be a big change for Peggy, but right now all she wanted was time with Jack.

Allie and Edward flew home to happy children, excided parents, and their peaceful farm.

The wife's had pocketed lots of money from their stay in N.Y. Abduls attorney, Moser Hasan Ahtam had given each of them fifty thousand extra. He then quit his practice and disappeared with his family to places unknown. Peggy was now in charge of Jaya's finances. It was a relieve to see that the attorney had not taken Jaya's money.

Peggy, Allie, and Gwynn would always come at a moment's notice, without pay, whenever Jaya needed them or maybe just for a visit. They were only a plane flight away.

Jaya was leaning back on big fluffy pillows in a comfortable chair on her private balcony. Her foot was propped up on a pillowed foot stool. This was her favorite spot to observe this famous American city. She was watching the lights twinkling in tall buildings all over the Big Apple. She could even see the shadowy treetops in Central Park fading with the setting of the sun.

She started thinking about all she had lived thru in her life. How amazing it was to be sitting here in this wonderful place, now. She was safe from violence and the manipulation of others. And she would be able to spare her children and the women that had become her family, the pain and hurt she had suffered.

Jaya thought about the note with its warning of Abduls' coming. It was just by chance she had received it and not Jamel.

She believed, Allah, had given her the chance to rid the world of Abdul the monster.

The bodyguards had been notified by the Imam's to kill Abdul and would pay the three men to do it. They would have gladly killed him for free.

The three felt loyalty to Jaya after watching how she treated everyone in her home. Jaya knew these men and their families. She had overheard the three talking about the difficulties of Abdul not paying their families, the money promised for the men's time in N.Y.C. She immediately gave them money to send home to their families. They had not asked for her help. She had marched out to them and handed an envelope to each one with more money than they had ever seen.

Jaya had two duffle bags of American money under her bed. She had taken them from Abduls safe room at the farm. She wished she had taken three bags!

When the guards received the message from the Imams to assonate Abdul, the three went to Jaya and explained what was going to happen. They told her to stay locked in her home.

She surprised them with her plan to take care of the body. Jaya told them she had been planning to kill Abdul herself and had already paid for his funeral. She did not mention to the guards the cremation. She did not want them to start thinking about Muslim Law. They were ready to kill him, but they would be uneasy about not following tradition in burial. After the assignation they would take care of delivering the body to the funeral home

Jaya then gave the three, fifty thousand each, from her private stash of money. The men could then go home to their families and make a new start. She was also assuring their silent with the extra payment.

Jaya had arranged the cremation of Abdul at a local funeral home with Afghanistan ties and a hate of Abdul. Abdul did not deserve any respect that traditions showed. He had never showed kindness or love of men, women, children, or country. His dust was to be emptied into the trash and then taken to a N.Y. land field.

Jaya's made her thoughts returned to ice skating lessons for she and the children. She also wanted to take the Flowers' and her children to Allies' farm. Allie had said that there was a large farm for sale, just down the road from hers. Jaya thought she would most likely buy it. She would keep the apartments for a while and then turn them over to Peggy too sale.

Taking revenge against evil and wining was a gift from God. Jaya was the winner.

www.ingramcontent.com/pod-product-compliance
Lightning Source LLC
Chambersburg PA
CBHW031026190726
48286CB00003BA/1043